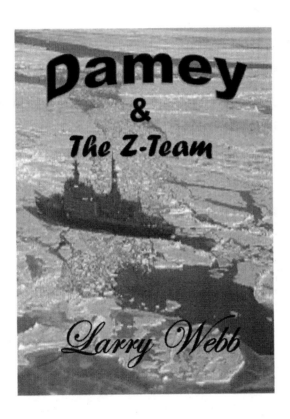

ALSO BY LARRY WEBB

The following books can be found at Amazon.com, Barnes & Noble.com, Schulers.com, and other online book sellers.

Damey & Grandpa Tutor
Taming Little Ike
Really Short Shorts—A book of short, short stories
Sometimes Home Ain't "Home Sweet Home"
As Life Goes On – Book one
As Life Moves On – Book two
As Life Continues—Book three

To get more information, go to www.larrywebb-author.com and read the descriptions.

ACKNOWLEDGEMENTS

I would like to recognize and thank three special people who put in a great deal of time and effort making this book possible. Without their editing, flow-checking, suggestions, and feedback, this novel would not be nearly what it is today. THANKS TOALL OF YOU.

Dr. Mary Anna Kruch, PhD, author of *Tend Your Garden: Nurturing Motivation in Young Adolescent Writer (FRAMEWORKS FOR WRITING)*

Jim Shirey, a long time court recorder and legal editor from Indianapolis, Indiana

Judy Hazelo, who has edited several of my books and is the one I always blame for any typos

Damey and The Z-Team
By
Larry Webb

PROLOGUE

Damey walked outside and squinted into the blinding sun. Shading his eyes, he turned around and looked at the sign one last time: LAMBERT, LAMBERT, AND HOTCHKISS, ATTORNEYS AT LAW. Thank God that's over, he thought. Little did he realize right then how much more stressful the notification of a will would affect him fourteen years later.

With a check tucked into his inner suit coat pocket, he turned and headed to the parking lot. His mind swirled like a dust devil. What were they going to do with all the money? His adoptive Grandpa Tutor— William "Bill" Berkley—had left him a bundle he didn't expect or deserve. Whatever they did with it, he had to make Grandpa proud.

Unlocking his sports car and climbing in, he thought maybe the time had come for him and his wife, Zandy, to buy a house. That's one of the things Grandpa suggested. He and Zandy had met at Dewline, a robotics engineering firm, three years previously, fell in love, and married. However, at that time in their lives, living in the condo was awfully easy. He had no lawn to mow, no snow to shovel, and the housekeeper cleaned the place. All he had to do was work, eat out most of the time, and finish his PhD in Robotics Engineering at Michigan State University. Zandy's masters in a combined computer science and electrical engineering degree from the same institution would be done in another couple of weeks. After that, they could relax and take life as it came—which figured to be a pretty laid back existence.

When he got back to his office at Dewline Engineering, he walked straight to his wife's work station. As the head of her own electrical engineering group, she typically could be found in her office buried behind her computer or on the floor looking over her crew's shoulders at whatever robot they were currently working on. He couldn't find her.

Damey walked up to one of the engineers in her group. "Where's Zandy?"

"She left about an hour ago. Said she had some kind of an appointment. Didn't say what. Didn't say when she'd be back."

"Well, when she does, please tell her I'm looking for her," Damey said.

Damey wandered back to his office and booted up the computer. He had one major project in the works keeping his brain spinning. His goal was to develop a robot that would work underwater and crawl along the ocean floor with cameras and recording devices for oceanographers studying marine life, ecosystems, and ocean currents.

He had a number of other projects in the pipeline, but Damey thought they were going to be so easy, the time and energy spent on them would almost be boring. He'd let his staff handle most of them. Others were in the contract stage and hadn't been scheduled for development yet. What he really needed at that point was for the mechanical and electrical people to get a couple more of the robots physically built so he could get serious with the testing and operational phases. It was either that, or he needed a real challenge.

Damey sat there and stared at the screen, but he couldn't concentrate. Instead, he leaned back in his chair, put his feet up on the desk, folded his hands behind his head, and stared off into space, amazed at how far he'd gone, remembering where he'd come from.

***

My God, what a wild and crazy life I've led, and I'm only twenty-three. I grew up in poverty and didn't even realize it. Mom worked at a menial job in an insurance company and went to school in the evenings and on weekends to eventually get her RN. The stay-at-home moms in the low-income housing project where we lived kept an eye on all of us kids. We were like a big community all of our own. There was a handful of dads around, but not many. Most families consisted of single mothers and kids.

My life never really changed that much until we moved into a Habitat for Humanity house at the beginning of summer vacation when I was eleven. That's when my neighbor, William Berkley, who evolved into being my Grandpa Tutor, took over my education and spent the summer and next school year tutoring and teaching me everything he thought I should know. He was a retired school teacher and figured all those "Donation Ds" I received as a sixth grader didn't cut it. Wow! By the end of the seventh grade I made the "B" honor roll. After that, I earned all As. Don't know how I did it, but eventually I ended up with three male mentors in my life, and it was like good grades were expected—not only by them, but me as well.

After almost a year with Grandpa Tutor taking charge of my life and education, another man came onto the scene. Mom met my middle school gym teacher at parent-teacher conferences, and they clicked. After a hectic year and a half, he ended up as my dad. I couldn't love a father more than I do him. The first thing I did when they told me about their engagement was to beg him to adopt me. Standing in front of the judge when he hit that little wooden block with his gavel making it official had to be the happiest single moment of my life. I cried like a baby.

To make my life even weirder, that's the same time period when I met Xavier, the sperm donor. I don't respect him enough to recognize him as my biological father, so that's what I call him. The last thing I'd ever call him is Dad. However, I sure had a number of other choice words to call him during our relatively brief relationship. Wonder who hates whom more, him or me?

A little later Sam came out of nowhere and entered my life as another mentor. God, what a character. I love him to pieces, but sometimes he drives me nuts. Towards the end of my junior year in high school, our robotics team won the state competition. I acted as spokesman for our group and explained our project to the judges. I guess that's why he picked me out of the crowd. I still remember it like it was yesterday. After all the presentations, this complete stranger walked up to me.

"My name is Sam Wardwell. I own Dewline Robotics Engineering. Here's my card with my number

and company address. Tomorrow is Saturday. Be at my office in the morning at nine o'clock sharp."

Typical Sam, he didn't even tell me why. At nine a.m. the next morning I knocked on his office door. He showed me around the place, talking non-stop. Two hours later I left with the paperwork to take to school to get my working permit. He didn't even ask me if I wanted the job. It was like I didn't even have a choice. He told me I had to go to work every day during the school week from three to six and on Saturdays from eight to twelve. My job entailed following around his engineers, do everything they told me to do, and learn absolutely everything. I don't know why, but my first check came as a complete surprise. I didn't even know I was getting paid. We'd never talked about that. As soon as school dismissed for the summer, I worked five hours a day, six days a week. Vacation? Forget it. There was too much for me to do and learn. I didn't even have time for a quick weekend get-away to Lake Michigan.

I still think the craziest thing Sam ever did happened during summer break between my sophomore and junior years at MSU. He put me on a plane to Atlanta with orders to go fix a problem they had with a robot at some small manufacturing plant. He gave me a week to take care of the situation before he would "...feel obligated to send somebody who knows what they are doing."

Two sixteen hour days later, I'd resolved the issue and improved their system to boot. Naturally, Sam gave me hell when I showed up the next day because he'd wanted me to go out on the town, see Atlanta in the evenings, and have some fun. I didn't. I flew back. The thing is, he'd never told me that part of the deal. Didn't matter. He still yelled at me before giving me a bonus because I exceeded his expectations.

So here I am, seven years later with a BS, MS, and a healthy start on my PhD, all in robotics engineering, all thanks to Sam who has paid for the majority of it and lives by the credo, "Damey, we've got a problem in Waco, London, Toronto, Miami, or wherever. Here's your ticket. Your plane leaves tomorrow morning. And, oh yeah, don't forget to tell Zandy."

***

A half hour later Zandy walked in, "Hi, honey. How did the reading of the will go? You get Grandpa's watch like you figured you might?"

"No," Damey said as he pulled the check out of his pocket and dropped it on the desk in front of her. "Look at this."

"Holy crap! Didn't expect anything like that. What are you going to do with it?"

"Not me, we. What are *we* going to do with it? You know Grandpa. The first ten percent goes in our retirement account, and the next ten goes to savings," he said laughing. "He suggested a couple of things like us paying off our college loans, of which we don't have any thanks to Sam. He also mentioned finishing my PhD and buying a house. But, like he stipulated in the will, the money is ours to do with whatever we want."

"Before we get all carried away with plans for a new yacht or vacation home on the Rivera, I've got some news for you too. I had a doctor's appointment this afternoon."

"Why? How come I didn't know anything about it? Is something wrong? Is there something you haven't told me?"

"I'm two months pregnant."

Damey jumped out of his seat and planted his lips on Zandy's mouth. They squeezed each other in a deep hug as tears ran from their eyes. They'd been trying since they married two years ago.

CHAPTER 1

Fourteen years later, Damey sat at his desk lost in thought. There were a couple of things he wasn't happy about. His underwater robot could smell and detect oil and other foreign materials, but he didn't feel confident about the tracking device yet. The buzzer on Damey's desk beeped twice. He took a deep breath, got out of his seat, and headed to Sam's office. He really didn't really want to be distracted right then. Over the years Damey had learned that if the buzzer beeped twice, one of Sam's so-called emergencies had arrived. If it beeped three times, run! As vice president of Dewline, Sam expected Damey to be able to solve all his problems right off the top of his head.

Damey walked down the hall still thinking about the latest glitch in the system. "Yeah, Sam. What's up?" he asked when he walked through the doorway. He really didn't want to know.

"We might have received the break we've been looking for to blow Dewline into a worldwide robotics super power. I just now finished talking to someone at the Department of Defense. There appears to be some kind of an oil leak under the ice shelf in the Antarctica. Drilling there is illegal so if there is something going on, it's against the international treaty banning all gas, oil, and mineral exploration," Sam said.

A series of international agreements starting with the Antarctic Treaty was signed originally in 1959, culminating in 1998 with a revision of the Madrid Protocol which banned all commercial mineral exploration and mining until 2048 when the policy will be reexamined.

"Trying to pump oil out of there would be crazy," Damey said. "It would cost more to get it out of the ground and transport it to a refinery than what it's worth. They couldn't sell it. At the price of oil today, traditional companies are struggling."

Damey fought with himself to keep from rolling his eyes. He knew exactly where this conversation was headed. He'd had these talks with Sam way too often for his liking. He was going on another one of Sam's "little trips." His boys hated it when he was gone. It was going to be another tough night at home.

"Not our problem. The Department of Defense called and asked how we were coming on our underwater robot. I gave him the basics and told him I thought we were ready to at least give it a whirl."

"How'd they know about it? We haven't said a word publicly. It's been a secret project."

"I didn't ask—they didn't offer. All I did was volunteer your services, and they need them *now*. They're bringing in a cargo plane to Capitol City International Airport this afternoon. No more experimenting in mud puddles; you're flying out in the morning. Grab your crew and get that monstrous thing ready for them to pick up. Might want to finish that 'tweak' you were complaining about first. Don't wait for your team to figure it out, just go ahead and do it yourself."

"Oh, thanks," Damey said giving Sam a dirty look before laughing. Goofy old Sam would never change— 'Just do it.'

Still smiling because of Sam's complete oblivion of his sarcasm, Damey asked, "So, you say they think it's somewhere under an ice shelf. Which Sea—the Ross or the Weddell? Is that where they're looking or do we have a different destination?"

"It's seeping out from under the Weddell ice shelf. They know that much. After that, it's a mystery. They have no clue where it's coming from. What we need to do is load you and your magical, oil sniffing, underwater robot on the transport plane and go find it.

"Before you do, however, isn't it the underwater welding device that you have to look at? Can you get the water in the vat down to sub-zero temperatures this

15

afternoon so you can make sure it works if you start right now?"

"Yeah, I can. So, you think I can just go out there and find the leak when the Navy can't?" Damey asked.

"That's the plan. That baby will sniff out the oil and follow it to its source—whatever it is. Ain't robotics cool? One more thing. You know that new aramid fiber tow rope and reel we picked up that's supposed to be literally indestructible? You might want to attach that to the front of the robot too. Place it close enough to the claws so they can attach it to whatever.

"I don't know what you'd use it for, but better to have it and not need it than the other way around. Besides, if you get the chance, it might be a good way to test it. It's supposed to be resistant to salt water and other chemicals, temperature extremes, and still be able to handle heavy loads without breaking. Be interesting to see if it's as good as advertized."

"Like I haven't anything better to do this afternoon but hook up a tow rope. Sam, you and your bright ideas. Checking the welder and getting it ready to ship isn't enough? I'll have one of the guys do it. And, oh yeah, by the way, have you informed Zandy of this wonderful mission you volunteered me for yet? Is she going too since she's the head of computer programming around here?"

"No, and telling her is your job. Zandy and the rest of the Z-Team are staying here to hold down the home front. Seriously, I wouldn't do that to the boys. I couldn't send both of you on this one even if I would like to. I know, their grandparents would be more than happy to take care of them, but this could be hazardous. They need their mom at home with them for moral support while they wait for you to do your magic."

"Hummm! Maybe I should give Zack a call at school and see if he wants to come by this afternoon for a chat?" Damey said trying to keep a straight face.

"You keep Zachary away from me. One of his cranky tirades a year is enough."

"That wasn't this year," Damey said. "It was in December, which makes it last year."

"Yeah, right. You wait until tonight to tell him. Oh, another thing. You've got to swear Zandy, the boys, and your parents all to secrecy. If they hear something from you that isn't on the news, they cannot say anything about it," Sam said. "The guy from the Secretary of Defense's office couldn't stress that point enough. The whole mission is top secret. They don't think any of the other countries who have research stations in the Antarctic are even aware of it, and they want to keep it that way."

CHAPTER 2

Damey hustled out of Sam's office and straight to Zandy's. He walked in, checked to make sure none of her co-workers were in there, and closed the door. "We need to talk."

He explained the situation to her the best he could. Both understood this was something he *had* to do.

"You're responsible for telling those paranoid munchkins of yours tonight," Zandy said.

"Mine. They're half yours too."

"Yeah, right. Look in the mirror."

"All kidding aside," Damey said, "we've got to make them understand I have to go. I'm the only one who can do this since we've only trained it to react to my voice commands. Wish this was happening six months from now. Oh, yeah. There's also the national security concern as well. They can't even tell their cousins or any of their other friends."

Zandy took a deep breath. "Let's wait until after dinner and tell them before our bike ride. We'll sit the three of them down on the sofa where we can stand beside each other and tell them the truth."

"You know, of course, we're setting up the entire night to be a disaster."

"What other choice do we have? You're leaving in the morning."

18

The rest of the day was a whirlwind of activity—tweaking and testing the welder in sub-zero temps, attaching the winch and aramid fiber tow rope, and getting everything ready to load and ship.

With the weather and iceberg filled waters, the Weddell Sea is considered by some to be the most dismal and treacherous place known to man. Between the winds, currents, and nasty temperatures, it's not a place most people would want to visit, much less work.

Sam walked into Damey's work area. "The Navy cargo plane just landed over at the Capital City International Airport. The guys who took the first load of supplies over to the hanger just called. They've seen at least four armed guards and two German Shepherds."

"Oh, great. The media will have a field day with that—especially after we back up our big truck to it, throw the tarps over the opening, and load the plane. Can't you just hear them?"

An hour and a half later, they had to fight their way through traffic to get to the terminal with the truck. When they backed the truck up to the back of the plane, Zandy said, "Look at the gawkers. People must have spotted that huge plane and *had* to come get a look to see what's going on."

"Good luck with that," Damey answered. "With the precautions we've taken, no one will have a clue. It's too bad people can't get closer to get a good look at that huge thing, but because of security, that's the way it's got to be."

Newsmen armed with running cameras screamed over the fence. "Excuse me. Excuse me, but can you tell us what's going on?"

No one from the plane's side of the fence answered.

Like Damey had said, all anyone could see were one huge and two smaller unmarked trucks pull onto the tarmac and park behind the back of the plane. One at a time, they backed up to the gaping opening at the back of the plane. The tarps they'd set up at the plane's back end prevented anyone on the other side of the fence from seeing anything.

"Everybody ready?" Damey asked when everything had been loaded. They had three vehicles that they'd parked behind the plane to help defy detection. "When we drive out of the airport, Sam, you turn left on Airport Road, and then make another left on Grand River. Zandy and I'll turn right. Fred, you turn left on Airport road and then turn right on Grand River. The military police from the local National Guard unit have been assigned to block all exits for fifteen minutes after we leave so no one can follow us back to Dewline. Let's hope nobody thought to photograph the license plates."

"No sweat. I had the guys cover the plates with wrapping paper," Sam said. "Besides, if the media people do figure it out, we'll just tell them it's a national security issue. If they want any details, they can call the National Security Agency in DC. We did all we could do to keep things a secret."

Zandy looked over at him. "Let's hope nobody recognizes you. You're the best known commodity around here. Somebody might."

"That's why I'm wearing sunglasses as well as this hat with the brim pulled down over my eyes."

"I wondered about that," Zandy said with a smile. "Looks a little goofy on you—like Joe Superspy or something."

That evening Damey and Zandy waited until the boys finished their clean-up detail after dinner to say anything. Before they headed out on their nightly family bike ride, Damey took a deep breath, held it, and then spoke. "Hey, guys, Mom and I want to talk to you. Come into the living room and sit down."

Damey and Zandy had decided to play it cool and not to make a big deal out of it. They'd tell the kids up front what was going on.

"What'd we do wrong?" eleven year-old Zane asked. He was not only the youngest of the three, but the most vocal. He was also the most suspicious, figuring a directive like that from Dad usually meant they were in trouble."

"Nothing. How's that for starters? We want to tell you about something that came up at work this morning that the three of you may not be real happy about. Oil has been spotted floating to the surface from under the ice somewhere down in Antarctica. Drilling for oil there is illegal, so they're hoping it's a natural leak. Right now, nobody knows for sure what the source is."

"No!" Zack exploded. "You're not gonna go find that thing. No way. You just had another one of those *business trips* a couple of months ago. Why can't somebody else do it this time? Why's it always gotta be you? Not fair! No! Less we can go with you like we did on that trip in July to the Oklahoma oil fields?" At thirteen, Zachary, normally the quietest of the three, also tended to be the angriest and most emotional.

"No, you can't go, but I have to. The US Department of Defense has asked Dewline to help, and the new underwater robot which reacts to voice commands is my deal. Right now, I'm the only one it obeys. Hopefully, it won't be for more than a few days. Look, guys, none of us are happy about this, but we have to put our country's interest and security first. If someone is drilling illegally, it could have international repercussions."

"Yeah, like what?" Zack muttered. "ISIS going to sink your ship?"

"No, nothing like that. There could be a lot of political fallout, but nobody's going to start a war over this," Damey answered, hoping he was telling the truth.

The crestfallen looks on the boys' faces told the story. They didn't believe for a minute that it would only be for a couple of days. They hated having their dad gone. The close, tight-knit family did not do well when separated—any of them.

Zandy looked over her brood and shook her head. The boys acted just like she and Damey had figured they would. "There's another issue here, boys, and Dad and I cannot emphasize this enough. Anything dealing with this trip that is not covered by the media is top secret. You cannot even tell your cousins or friends where Dad is or what he's involved with unless it shows up on TV or in the paper. You can tell them he's gone on a business trip, but that's all. You *have* to play dumb. As far as you're concerned, it's just another one of those darned trips that you hate because he's gone so often. Just don't forget, *everything* is top secret because the government doesn't know WHAT is going on. Understand?"

Staring at the floor, all three nodded and grunted that they did.

"When are you leaving?" Zaiden asked with his lips curled down looking like he was about ready to fall apart emotionally.

At twelve-years-old, Zaiden suffered the same major problem as his brothers—dealing with puberty and all the mental and emotional turmoil involved with that. All three would find themselves crying for no reason and having no idea why they were doing it, which, of course, drove their parents crazy. Sitting together on the sofa, each boy wiped his eyes and cheeks periodically with his shirt sleeve.

"The government sent a military cargo plane to the airport, and they've already loaded it. My team got everything all set up this afternoon and ready to go. Tomorrow morning a military vehicle from the National Guard will pick me up at Dewline and take me through a private entrance at the back of the airport and on to the tarmac where the plane is parked. I'll slip in the door facing away from the viewing area.

"As soon as I go over the inventory list and then double-check it to make sure we have everything—like the stuff we added today, we'll take off. The plane will fly nonstop except for fueling to McMurdo Station in Antarctica. A helicopter will meet me there and fly me out to an icebreaker in the Weddell Sea. I assume that as long as there is progress, I'll stay."

"How long you think you'll be gone?" Zack asked.

"Honestly, I don't know. Hopefully, it won't be that long. Maybe just a few days."

"What's it like there?" Zane asked looking up red eyed.

"Should be nice. It's spring in that part of the world now. We'll be landing on a snow-covered runway at McMurdo. Their average daily high temperature for October is a balmy four degrees above," Damey said with a straight face. What he told them was true, but it was far from "balmy."

At that point, Zack stood, stomped up the stairs to his bedroom, slammed the door, threw himself on the bed, and cried himself to sleep. They forgot about the night's bike ride. Zane and Zaiden stuck to their parents like glue, asking question after question.

Damey sat down at the family room computer with the two of them in front of their thirty inch monitor while they researched the Antarctica. Didn't look like a fun place to hang out to any of them.

"Dad, what do they use Icebreakers for? They don't just cruise around breaking up ice, do they?"

"Well, I know in the Great Lakes the US Coast Guard uses them to keep shipping lanes open in the winter. Sometimes cargo ships hauling iron ore and other things get stuck in the ice unexpectedly," Damey answered.

"Wonder how long the guys have to stay on them. Wouldn't want to have to be on one of those things for a long time. It's too darned cold to be able to do anything," Zane said.

"I don't know. Let's ask Ma Google," Damey said.

They poked around on the Internet for a while and finally found a couple of US Coast Guard icebreakers they could look at.

"Eight months? No way. That'd be terrible. There'd be nothin' to do," Zaid said.

"According to this, they have lounges, libraries, gymnasiums, and a store. I'm sure it isn't all bad," Damey said.

While Damey and the boys explored the Internet, Zandy called Damey's parents, Ty and Shaundra Williams, and explained the situation to them. Grandpa Williams, who was also the middle school's boys' gym teacher, said he'd meet the boys at the door of the school in the morning.

Later that evening after the two younger boys went to bed, Damey went upstairs, slipped into Zack's room without waking him, took off his clothes, rolled him over onto his left side in his normal sleeping position, tucked him in, and kissed him goodnight. Standing over his son watching him breath, he sighed. He wasn't happy either.

None of the family slept soundly that night. Damey and Zandy both heard Zack get up around two and use the bathroom before going back to bed. The other boys kept turning from one side to the other and squirmed for what seemed to Damey and Zandy, the entire night.

Breakfast was so uncharacteristically quiet that it felt like a trip to the city morgue. Damey understood, but missed the non-stop chatter. It felt almost like the kids were ignoring him. However, when he dropped them off at school, he got three tight hugs and more tears.

Grandpa Williams was waiting at the door and met the boys when Damey dropped them off so he could hustle them to his office. After getting everybody settled down and faces washed, he sent them off to class, letting them know they could always bail out at any time and run to his office in the gym. If they faced a meltdown, he'd be there for them.

Ty smiled. Some things never changed, he thought. Years previously he'd had Damey in class and on his wrestling team even before he'd become his dad. He'd had to handle a few of his emotional traumas as well. The time had flown by way too quickly.

CHAPTER 3

A day later, the naval aircraft landed on the snowy Antarctic runway at McMurdo. While Damey and the crew took a twelve-hour break for dinner and rest, the crew unloaded the robot and computer system and attached it to the bottom of one of the base's helicopters.

The USCGC LaGoon, a large, outdated—soon-to-be mothballed icebreaker, had space for two helicopters on deck and only one of them was being used at the time. As soon as Damey's ride sat down, the ship's commander, Captain Morissy, greeted him with a stiff handshake and a straight, unsmiling face.

"Surprised they sent a civilian. I'd of thought they'd send a Navy underwater demolition crew in case there really is an oil rig down there," Morissy said.

"This is the newest and most advanced technology in the world," Damey said. "No Navy personnel have been trained on it yet. They wouldn't know how to run it. Right now, only the other engineers and computer scientists at Dewline and I know the programming language we created for this thing. It's unique to this robot. Another little issue we haven't resolved yet is the fact that it only follows my voice commands. As you can see, we've got more work to do on it, but this is what we have. Hopefully it'll get the job done."

"Yeah, right," Captain Morissy said. "What do you need from us?"

"First off, I need some people to carry my computer and command center materials to one of the upper bridges where I can set up a work station attached to the ship's computers. The higher up the better. What I would really like is to have it in the navigation room from where you operate the ship. Can I connect to the ship's computers from there?"

"Yeah, that's not a problem," Morissy said. "Then what?"

"Then, I'll need however many men it takes to support and move the device. I need it unhooked from the body of the helicopter and set over close to the edge of the ship. It took six men to lift and attach it to the bird. As soon as it's removed, the pilot wants to raise the chopper and head back to McMurdo."

"He was bitching about something over the intercom shortly after you got here," Morissy said. "I think he's cold and wants to get back to McMurdo where he can warm up. Must be it's cold up there on that chopper when the engine's turned off. Poor guy."

"While they're doing that, maybe you can back the icebreaker up to get us into more open water. Have to be able to get the robot in the water and not set it on the ice. Once we're free of this ice jam, your crew can gently ease it down into the water and secure it to the ship until I'm ready. "

"That robot of yours looks like it has hands," Morissy said after he'd given the command to dislodge the ship from the ice and back up to a little more open water.

"It does. If we find an oil rig down there, this thing can weld a seal around the leak and could probably disable the well if the government wants to. It's pretty versatile. If it's oil oozing out of the ground, then, that's a different issue. Don't know what we'll do then."

"You have any idea how cold it is down there? No way could you get the metal hot enough to weld over a leaky hole in some rig."

"*You* have no idea how hot a nuclear battery-generated flame can get either," Damey said trying hard not to sound condescending. If the Navy captain wanted to be a jerk, he could be as well. Their working relationship was not getting off to a good start.

As the icebreaker's personnel moved the devices into position under the watchful eyes of Damey and Captain Morissy, they talked gathering information from one another.

"Any ideas about what direction the oil flow is coming?" Damey asked.

"It appears to be flowing from under the ice right about where we are now facing which is due southeast. It's impossible to determine from here for sure because of water currents. The Belgrano 11 Base research station is straight ahead," Morissy said. "The leak could be somewhere between here and there or someplace totally different. Who knows at this point? The only thing I know for sure is that we're getting oil from someplace."

"That's the sweet thing about this robot. It can not only smell and detect oil and follow the scent like a bloodhound to the source wherever it happens to be, but it's also intuitive enough, it can more-or-less think for itself. At least, it's to the point where all I have to do is monitor its movements and give it suggestions once in awhile if I think it needs them.

"Once it finds the source of the leak, I'll turn on the camera and it will send us back a live view of whatever it sees on my monitor." Damey said. "From here, it'll look like we're riding on the back of the robot."

"Yeah, but how can it work under there? Anything you put down there will freeze over with ice almost instantly and disable it. Let's not forget just how extreme the water temperatures are down there. Also, let's not forget, we've been parked in twenty or more feet of ice."

"OK, but let's keep in mind what's driving this thing. The power source is a new, experimental, nuclear-powered water-based battery. The ionic solution used is not easily frozen even at extremely low temperatures. Makes it longer lasting, stable, and more powerful than the human mind can comprehend. Not only that, but I've programmed it so part of the energy from the battery will keep the outside body of the robot heated so ice won't form on it.

"It should be perfect for the job—at least that's what I'm counting on. I know the sensors can detect deposits of oil and other minerals underwater in the lab, but, unfortunately, it hasn't been tested in these conditions.

"We've done a lot of underwater testing in sub-zero situations, so if it works here like it has in trial runs, it will detect the oil flow and follow it to its source."

"So, why's this thing look so weird?" Morissy asked.

"We designed it to look like a prehistoric underwater sea creature on purpose. Some of them apparently survived because they could detect foreign materials. Strange as the thing looks, all of its parts are functional. The antennae are two cameras that work together or separately, the claws are extendable out to twenty feet and will grasp, laser cut, or weld from either claw. Those feet like things are stabilizers keeping it from tipping over in the water and can be used for slow motion crawling across the surface. Then, the nose is the sensor for oil, minerals, or anything else foreign to its environment—even the steel ships and planes are made of.

"Seems like our biggest problem right now is getting Hector, that's what one of my kids named the thing, tested and completely operational before any of our competitors do. That's why this excursion is important to our company as well as our country. I think we're there. What we haven't tried yet is using satellite coordinates to aid the sensing devices in search of places to explore for oil. That's next on the agenda off the coast of Texas."

"You mean there are actually other corporations out there doing the same thing? Why?"

"There's a huge market for it. If our robot can roam land or sea and find the best places to drill, it'll double the size of our company overnight. Something, I might add, I'm not nearly as wild about as our owner because every time there's a problem, he sends me. He seems to forget we have a hundred other engineers there who are perfectly capable.

"Anyway, we've got several land-based versions of this particular robot working in the oil fields in Oklahoma right now. Last summer when I had to go there on family business, I contacted a number of companies and started working with them. Not only will the land-based one find the oil closest to the surface, but it will help erect much of the drilling apparatus."

"Any other uses for the underwater version?" Morissy asked.

"Sure. We haven't gone looking yet, but our goal is to be able to find planes that have crashed in the oceans, ships that have gone down, and it has all kinds of possibilities for deep sea exploration for marine biologists and others."

"Captain, Dr. Williams, everything is in place," Guardsman Chappel said after walking up to them, popping to attention and saluting his commander.

"Good," Damey said. "Let's get started. First off, you might not like this, but I've got to connect the robot's computers to the ship's. The computers have to work together to automatically adjust to ship position, height differentiations, forward and lateral movement, tide, and any other conditions that might show up. "

"You're right, I'm not so sure I like that idea," Morissy said. "Will the robot's computers have the ability to take over the ship?"

"No, no. They just have to be synchronized."

Damey and the captain walked up to the navigating bridge where they directed the crew in the placement of his computer. It took a while, but Damey connected it to the ship's main operating system as well as the emergency backup systems. After they set up spare desk space, seating arrangements, and a work station for Damey, he fired up his computer and went to work.

Captain Morissy asked. "You're not plugged in anyplace other than being connected to the ship's computers. What are you using for power?"

"That's all built into the system. The nuclear power system running the robot also runs the computers. It's all part of the synchronizing process. That makes it a little more reliable and self-sufficient. You might not have noticed, but we pulled the plugs on the ship's computers as soon as I went operational. They are all now running off the current produced by my equipment. That way, we don't have to worry about the ship losing power."

"Yeah, right. Well, that's not gonna happen," Morissy said with an edge to his voice.

Watching over Damey's shoulders, all Morissy could see was a myriad of 1s and 0s and a jumble of other programming code that made absolutely no sense to him. The mouse's arrow popped all over the screen while Damey set things up.

"Thought it had a brain so it would run itself?" Morissy said.

"It does, more or less, once I finish programming the robot's computer, and everything is coordinated and synchronized. After all the basic directions and goals are keyed in, it kind of takes over the search and operates as instructed. I have to monitor it continually and reset its brain if it wanders too far off course. I can tell it to switch gears and go left or right orally. My goal is that one day I can just talk to it, tell it what I want it to do, and then sit back and watch it do its thing. Right now it still requires some manual directions even though most of what you'll observe will be oral."

"That'd be scary. With that kind of technology, some freak could take over the world."

"I know, and I'll bet by the time my kids get out of college, the technology will be there."

"How old are your kids?"

"Thirteen, twelve, and eleven," Damey said never taking his eyes off the screen.

"Don't even want to think about that," Morissy said and walked out of the door of the steering station bridge. The whole idea of computers that smart and powerful freaked him out.

While he was gone, the seamen monitoring and controlling the ship's functions spent a lot of their time chatting with Damey. They were intrigued with the new technology being developed and wanted to hear about it. Whenever the captain came back, they'd shift back behind their own work stations and keep quiet.

Morissy checked back for the third time several hours later. This time he noticed a double screen-shot, showing on Damey's sixty inch monitor. One side showed a red line tracing back and forth under the sea, and the other side consisted of rolling computer code.

"How's it going?" the captain asked.

"Good, except it's not sensing the exact direction the flow is coming from yet. See these little blips on the screen? That's where it detects oil. Then it loses the scent and drifts off. Think of it like a search and rescue dog looking for a lost child. Kind of works the same. It responds to the scent but takes commands from its owner. If the person it's following walks into a river, the dog loses the scent. When he gets to the other side, he may or may not pick up the scent again. That's where I come in. When Hector gets too far off course, I auto-correct his heading to the blips on the radar screen that indicate oil. At least so far, the robot has been able to find the scent again every time after it's lost it. I'm betting ocean currents are raising havoc with the oil stream. They are probably dispersing the flow of the oil as soon as it leaks out of the well, ground, or wherever it's coming from. This might take a while."

Around three in the morning, Damey took off his coat, rolled it up like a pillow, lay down on the floor, and fell asleep.

CHAPTER 4

Damey slept fitfully. Naturally, he had to dream of home and his family. He dreamed about Dewline closing down for two weeks over the holidays last winter so people of all faiths could enjoy a respite with their families. Sam Wardwell, the owner, treated it as paid vacation time. Friday evening before they locked the doors, Dewline had had their annual "Winter Break" party.

All the employees and their families looked forward to the party, the break, and their annual bonus checks, which were also distributed after the party. Sam loved the concept of profit sharing and surprises. He thought it motivated everyone and made them work harder. Therefore, nobody ever knew how much to expect until he handed them their checks. Even though most employees used direct deposit for their pay, the bonus check was always just that—a printed check hand delivered by the boss. That's what he wanted, and that's what he got.

After dinner and a couple more hours of socializing with live music being played in the background, people began rounding up their families. When the first family headed to the closet area for their coats, it signaled that the party was over. Everyone else would then get around and call it a night. That's when Sam positioned himself near the door so he could pass out the checks.

That's when Damey's vivid dream went to the next level. Not realizing it, he smiled into his pillow and watched the scene unfold.

"Damey, what is Zachary doing?" Zandy asked. She turned her head towards the far corner of the room near the door and nodded.

He looked where she was pointing and scowled. "Right now, I'd say he's standing toe-to-toe with our boss, fists doubled up and shoved into his sides, red faced, mad as hell, and yelling."

"Yeah, that was kind of my take on the situation. People are watching them and laughing. You'd better go over there and get the brat before he gets us both fired."

"Be right back." Damey watched himself hustle to the corner of the room where the two of them were still going at it. "Zachary, what on earth are you doing?"

"Back off, Damey. This is between Zack and me," Sam said.

"Dad, it's okay. I'm keeping my cool."

"Didn't look like it to me from the other side of the room, but you'd better be, or your thirteen year-old butt will be grounded until you graduate from med school."

Damey watched himself slowly shake his head and amble back to his wife.

"So, what's going on over there?" Zandy asked.

"I have no clue. Both of them more-or-less told me to get lost."

Damey rolled over on the floor, fluffed up his coat like he would his pillow, and went back to his deep slumber as the dream picked up where it had left off.

Five minutes later the standoff ended. Damey and Zandy watched Zack and Sam shake hands and separate—neither one smiling. Zack headed over to the desert table where he snagged another piece of cake and more lemonade. As could be expected, the younger versions of the Z-Team joined him.

Mom and Dad watched Zaiden and Zane trying to pump their brother for information. Still unsmiling, the eldest sibling shook his head, grabbed his third piece of cake for the night, and walked away.

"This is not exactly how I expected our holiday party to end," Damey said frowning.

Zandy just closed her eyes and shook her head. "If he eats any more cake and lemonade, his sugar high will keep him awake all night. Just what we need—an angry, agitated, wide-awake kid."

So, what was supposed to be not only their annual party, but a special celebration for Damey, Zandy and their crew for developing and creating a new, state-of-the-art nuclear, underwater robot ended up as a confrontation between their kid and the boss. After that, celebrating was the last thing on his mind. He wanted to get home and find out what had happened.

The five of them left shortly afterwards. When they shook hands with Sam and pocketed their checks, Damey couldn't help but notice the smirk on Sam's face when he shook hands with Zack as he hauled him in for a quick hug while ruffling the top of his head with the other hand. Sam whispered something into the boy's ear. Zack smiled.

When they pulled into the garage, Zandy told Zaiden and Zane to go to the family room and play computer games or go to bed. It was just about their normal bed time, but she didn't want them to think they were being punished because of their brother so she gave them a little slack.

Following orders, Zack parked himself in on the loveseat in the living room, folded his arms and rested his elbows on his knees. He stared at the floor and didn't look up. He waited. He knew he was in big trouble.

Standing straight with their backs arched slightly backwards in front of him, both parents folded their arms across their chests more-or-less mocking him and paused as they looked down. Zack didn't look up.

"Okay, spill it. What happened in there? That was our boss you were yelling at," Damey said after waiting a few seconds.

"Didn't yell. Maybe got a little excited, but kept my cool."

"What was it all about?"

"Can't tell ya."

"Wait a minute, young man," Zandy interrupted. "Let's not forget who you're talking to. We are your parents, and you will tell us what's going on—that is, unless you'd like to spend the rest of the weekend in your room thinking things over."

"Not fair."

"Why?" Damey asked. "Unless you explain yourself, that's exactly what's going to happen."

"Mr. Wardwell and I made a pact. We shook on it. What we talked about would be just between us. Not fair to punish me."

"You two actually agreed to keep us in the dark?" Damey asked.

"I don't like this one bit," Zandy said as she unfolded her arms and shifted her weight from one foot to the other. "I don't like the kids keeping secrets from us."

"Didn't do nothin' bad. I'd admit it if I did. Always do."

"*Yes, I'll give you credit for that one,*" *Zandy said softening a bit.*

She looked at Damey, raised her eyebrows, and shrugged her shoulders with that "Now what?" look on her face.

"*Go downstairs and play games with your brothers for a little while and burn off some of that sugar. Technically, it's past your bedtime so keep it low key,*" *Damey said.*

Zack scooted for the family room before Mom and Dad changed their minds.

Damey looked at Zandy and gave her a goofy look. What could they do? "You look at your check yet?"

"*No, they're both still in my purse. Let's take a peek.*"

CHAPTER 5

Captain Morissy walked onto the bridge early the next morning and spotted Damey asleep on the floor. "How long has he been there?"

"About three hours," one of the guardsmen answered. "We came on duty at midnight. We talked and watched him play around on the screen until he crashed around four. He's been dreaming and mumbling in his sleep ever since. Must be about something really weird. First he'll smile, and then he'll frown—back and forth he goes as he squirms around on the floor."

The sound of voices woke Damey from his reverie. He still had a smile on his face remembering the fiasco at the party with Zack's meltdown. He pushed himself to a sitting position and leaned against the wall as he refocused into wakefulness.

"Didn't anyone tell him where we stowed his gear? After all, we've turned over the smallest lounge down below to him, set up a bed and made it off limits to

everyone else until he's gone. It's not like we're
ignoring him."

"Have no clue, Sir. Nobody ever said anything
about it. He was working the monitor and then just kind
of sank to the floor and curled up in a fetal position
using his coat as a pillow and went to sleep. We figured
it best not to disturb him 'cause he appeared to fall
asleep as soon as he hit the deck."

"Doctor Williams, get up and let me show you your
quarters."

Still drowsy and only about half awake, Damey's
head popped up and looked at him with a dazed
expression. "Didn't realize I'd gone to sleep. I do need
a shower and shave though."

"You'd better get a few more hours rest first. I
looked at the screen and the red line is still moving
back and forth across the monitor."

Morrissy led Damey across the deck and down two
levels into the bowels of the ship. "This is actually kind
of an auxiliary lounge where guys can get away and be
by themselves. Nobody will bother you though 'cause
I've sent out a notice that the room's off limits. This
little hole in the wall over here is your private
bathroom, shower, and sink." He opened a door and
turned on a light to show him. Then he pointed out the
bed they'd set up for him.

Looking around, Damey spotted a small stash of
modern books the guys probably enjoyed along with a

sofa and chairs. It looked like a good place to get away from the stress up above and relax when he had the time.

"This will be your private quarters. After you rest up for a while, I'll show you the chow hall and the other lounges. When you're in here, you can lock the door if you want. Here on this nightstand is a charging station for cell phones, iPads, etc. Only problem is, you cannot use any of that stuff at this level on the ship. For instance, if you want to call home, you have to go to one of the lounges on the top deck or outside. It's a little chilly out there, but that's where you get the best reception.

"One other thing I guess I should tell you. Originally this room was used for ammunition storage. Therefore, it's probably the most secure room on the ship. As you can see, it's shaped like a big inverted V because it's the nose of the ship. The walls are very thick so it's almost impossible to hear anything going on outside of the room.

"In case of emergency, this room is also used temporarily as a brig. If someone commits a crime, we take them to McMurdo and things are sorted out there. If it's something simple like drunk and disorderly, we occasionally lock people up in here for a day or two—mainly to sober them up and give them a chance to sweat things out a while.

"What I'm trying to tell you is, we have an electronic locking system we control from topside. See these four slots in the door? They are the slide bolts that secure the room when needed. You don't have to worry about it though, there are only four of the upper echelon officers who know the code so nobody is going to play games and lock you in.

"Anyway, since the room is almost soundproof, you should be able to crawl into bed and have nothing bother you. You might hear the engines rumbling from below or maybe even feel them vibrate a little if we rev them up, but you shouldn't hear anything else. But, since we're stranded here until we figure out the oil problem, that isn't going to happen. So get some rest, and we'll see you in a few hours."

Damey looked longingly at the bed, kicked off his shoes, threw his clothes in the chair, and crawled in. He'd shave and shower when he woke up.

***

Damey once again fell into a dream state. It was after the holidays and winter break and the first day for Damey and Zandy to go back to work and the kids to school. Life had returned to normal.

Damey stared at his computer screen re-setting his brain for his robotics chores even while still thinking about Christmas and everything that had happened the past two weeks. The computers had all been kept running collecting data while they were gone. It'd take a week to analyze everything. On top of that, he had one-hundred and fifty emails to check. That's when his buzzer went off. Looking at his message, it said, "You and Zandy come to my office."

Oh, shit! Damey thought to himself as the long forgotten Friday evening fiasco from the party two weeks previously popped into his mind. No way can this be good.

When Damey and Zandy walked in, their boss sat at his computer looking at the corporate calendar.

"What's up, Sam?" Damey asked with a phony lilt to his voice as he tried to hide how he really felt. He shuffled a little from foot to foot and slipped his hands in his back pockets to keep them still. He didn't like stress, and now he knew they would have to address Zack's tantrum.

Sam looked up slowly from his computer with a slight frown on his face. "Zachary is going to Harvard Law School if I have to pay for it myself."

"He can't," Damey said laughing. Sam's remark about law school was a complete surprise and lifted the veil of tension. "We've already paid off his Michigan Educational Trust fund so college is already paid for as long as he goes to a Michigan school. Besides, he's a STEM guy at heart. He loves science, technology,

engineering, and math. I think all three of them are going to be robotics geeks like me."

"Okay, I'll compromise. He can go to the U of M law school."

"Blaspheme! Wash out your mouth with soap. He's going to MSU."

Zandy, who hadn't said a word yet, burst out laughing.

"Oh, get over it. Just 'cause you and Zandy went there doesn't mean the kids have to. He's getting double doctorates, robotics engineering and law. How's that for a combination? The second he passes the bar, he's coming to work for me. While he's in college, he can spend his summers here as an intern just like you did. In the mean time, get him on the debate team."

"Ah, does he have a choice in his life's career?"

"No," Sam said with a smile. "Not only that, but Zaiden's getting his PhD in robotics science along with an MBA, and Zane's getting his PhD in electrical engineering along with an MBA. Anyway, we'll deal with that down the road. We've got lots of time to fight over where they're going to college. The kid's educational future is not why I called you in here. Both of you come around the desk and look at the calendar on the screen. Pick out two weeks in June and two in August for your vacations."

"Sam, we only get four weeks a year. We just finished our two-week winter break, and we sometimes sneak in a week in the summer if work permits. This isn't going to add up. Besides, I want to ask you about what happened at the party."

"What? You were there. We had dinner, live music, people danced and socialized, and then everyone went home for the break."

"I'm talking about the fracas between you and Zack, and you know it."

"Sorry, Zack and I have a gentleman's agreement. We shook hands about keeping our discussion private and between us. You don't fit into the 'Need-to-know' category."

"Good grief! One of you is as bad as the other. I may have to beat it out of the kid."

"Yeah, right. Like you've ever laid a hand on him in anger. Now, like I said a minute ago, you two pick out four weeks for this summer. I'd prefer you split it up two and two, but if you insist, you can have four in a row."

"Are you serious?" Zandy asked.

Sam smiled and nodded.

Damey and Zandy leaned over the computer and marked the first two weeks of the kid's summer vacation and the last two.

Sam stood, faced Damey and Zandy with his fists doubled up and buried into his sides between the ribcage and the belt, scrunched his eyebrows together, skewed his mouth to the side to keep from laughing out loud and gave his well-practiced imitation of a squeaky, high-pitched, angry pubescent boy.

"This year's gotta be different. Since I've screwed you out of half of your vacations for as long as ANYONE can remember, and you never get to do nothin like go on a cruise or hike the Appalachian Trails or go to the Grand Canyon or Disney Land or Washington DC or nothin' else that takes time 'cause you always gotta get back to work and the stupid phone's always ringin' for work crap so you're still workin' when you're 'posed to be having fun. Can't even take a three-day weekend to Mammoth Cave without that phone goin' off continuously. So, leave the dumb thing home this summer and if Grandpa or Grandma wants to get a hold of you, they can call Zack's phone."

"Oh—my—God," Damey said wide-eyed as he slapped his forehead and burst out laughing. He and Zandy were both still laughing and shaking their heads as they walked out the door.

That night at dinner, Damey and Zandy told the boys. They had a job to do between then and June. Next summer they planned to spend one week in DC starting with the Smithsonian and what other sights they could

51

squeeze in, and then drive down to Tennessee and get on the Appalachian Trail for three to four days. It was up to them to research the journey.

Damey then put on a little show imitating Sam throwing his arms in the air exclaiming that they were getting four week's vacation that year since they'd been screwed out of their vacations for as long as anybody could remember.

Two of the boys laughed out loud. Zack dipped his head and looked up with sparkling eyes and the biggest smirk on his face that either Damey or Zandy had seen since before the party.

CHAPTER 6

A week after Damey left, the news of the suspicious oil leak finally showed up on television. The national broadcasts gave the details to date. Zandy and the boys stared at the screen without talking. The reporter announced that as soon as the US Navy became aware of the event, they had dispatched the closest ship to the area. It was the USCGC LaGoon, a heavy duty icebreaker complemented by a staff of four-hundred officers, Chief Petty Officers, and enlisted personnel. That would act as command center for the search.

Other ships, including a missile launching cruiser, cargo ship, destroyer, and four tugboats would be heading in that general direction. If the cause of the oil leak was a forbidden oil rig, the Navy planned to be ready in case of any repercussions. The operation's primary goal was to stop the leak. Damey and Dewline were not mentioned.

That made it all the more difficult for the boys because they all had social studies classes which discussed current events daily. For the most part, all they could do was sit and listen and not participate—which was not the norm for any of them. Usually their teachers had to shut them up so other kids could get a word in.

Jessie, Zack's best friend might have been the first to get a little suspicious. "You've been awfully quiet lately. What's going on?"

"Missing Dad, I guess. I hate it when he's gone. It drives me crazy."

"He's been gone before, and you've never acted like you are now. Anything to do with what we were talking about in class today?"

"He's on a business trip. They don't tell me everything," Zack said.

"Bull! Is he in the Antarctic?"

"Don't ask. I'm not a hundred percent sure of anything. Nothin' I can tell ya anyway. Hurry up. We're gonna be late for algebra. I gotta stop by my locker."

***

Damey woke up, rolled over on his pillow, looked at the clock on the bookshelf beside the bed, and then shut his eyes again. He should get up and check the computer's monitor. Hector could be bouncing against the side of an iceberg, and nobody would even know it.

Even though the room was supposed to be completely soundproofed, he could hear the diesel engines rumbling far below him. He felt a slight vibration from the motors. It lulled him back to sleep.

Two hours later, Damey crawled out of bed, shaved, jumped in and out of the shower, and got dressed in clean clothes. Before getting a bite to eat, he checked the computer. The robot seemed to be doing the same as earlier—getting a whiff of the oil, trying to track it, and then losing it. Nothing much had changed.

"Notice anything different?" Damey asked the two guardsmen monitoring the ship's controls.

"Nope, not a thing. What you see on the screen now is what we've seen the four hours we've been on duty. Back and forth, back and forth—nothing remotely interesting or different."

Damey looked at the time on his cell phone. It was eleven a.m. on the fifteenth. That meant it was five p.m. on the fourteenth at home. He punched number one on speed dial—Zandy.

True to form, the kids acted just like he figured they would. Zack sounded depressed and wanted his dad to come home. Zaiden told him all about the robot he was working on in his STEM class at school, and Zane was happy and bubbly as always—covering as many topics as he could in the short time they had.

Zandy told him about the news reports on TV and the fact that the media appeared to be downplaying the whole event into maybe nothing more than oil seeping out of the ground. She also let him know that neither he nor Dewline had been mentioned—driving their sons even "wackier than normal" because they couldn't share with their friends.

Damey missed Zandy and the kids as much as they missed him. It was hard to push the "End" button.

He stretched, twisted his shoulders back and forth, checked the monitor, gave the robot a couple of different oral commands, and then spoke to one of the crew members. "I'm going to run down to the mess hall and get something to eat. Can I bring you two back anything?"

Both indicated that they didn't want anything and would keep an eye on the monitor while he was gone. If anything different happened, they'd come and get him. They told him to take his time, eat, and enjoy himself.

After he went through the chow line, he looked around for a seat. The cafeteria was full. One table of lower ranking enlisted men had an empty seat. "Mind if I join you?" Damey asked.

"Sit down, Dr. Williams. Glad to have you."

"It's Damey. I hate being called doctor. I'm not going to check your pulse or your prostate."

Laughing, one of the seamen asked, "So, how's the search going? Any luck yet?"

"Nothing yet. When I go back, I plan to recalibrate Hector and see what I can come up with."

"Somebody said one of your kids named the thing. How'd that happen?"

"All my kids are computer and robotics geeks so have been following this particular robot from the beginning. I think their intrigued about how weird it looks and all the things it can do. Anyway, they sometimes come over after school for an hour or so if their grandpa is busy and can't watch them and then ride home with their mom. When they show up they come looking for Hector to see what we're doing with him that day.

"Zane, my youngest, came up with the name. He was watching me test something and popped up with, 'Tell Hector to grab it with both claws and do a one-eighty to see what breaks—his claws or the rod it's holding on to.' From then on, he's been know as Hector.

"So, anyway, I did what he suggested, and the rod broke. I'd never tried anything like that maneuver before, and it worked. Just goes to show, you're never too old to learn something new, even from an eleven-year-old."

The four at the table chatted for nearly an hour before all of them had to get back to work.

After lunch, Damey sat back down in front of the computer and started talking into the microphone and fiddling with the code.

Captain Morissy popped in and out during the day asking if there was anything Damey needed or if there was anything he could do. He felt uncomfortable having a civilian sitting in front of his computers, concerned that the guy could take over any of the ship's functions if he wanted to. It left him with a helpless feeling he didn't like, and there was nothing he could do about it.

Oblivious to Morissy and his paranoia, Damey changed tactics. He dropped the robot from its position of thirty feet below the bottom of the ice, where the oil flow seemed strongest, down to the ocean's floor and tried to pick up the scent of the oil from there. Traveling back and forth following a pattern like he was cultivating someone's farm, he strained his ears for that familiar pinging sound. Occasionally, he'd get a blip on the radar and try to follow it until it disappeared. Things looked a bit futile at times. Then something else would happen causing the adrenalin to surge, and then nothing.

It wasn't unusual to have four or five guardsmen standing behind, watching over his shoulders all staring at the screen looking for anomalies. "What's that blip just to the right and in front of Hector?" asked one of the onlookers.

"Beats me. Let's take a look." Damey turned on the searchlight and camera features in front of the robot and spotted a giant prehistoric looking creature bobbing along on the sea floor.

"What the hell is that thing?" a seaman asked.

"Just a second," Damey said. He pushed a couple of buttons and an 8 ½ X 11 glossy slid out of the lower part of his computer. "That's why I put in this camera and printer for just these occasions. Take this photo and see if you can Google the Antarctic and find out what it is.

Within a half hour the guardsman returned. "It's a giant sea pig or sea cucumber. They feed off the bottom and are fairly common. Looks to me like this one is a lot bigger than normal. Can I keep the picture? I want to scan it and email it to my kids at home."

"Sure," Damey said. "Anyone else want a copy? Since it has nothing to do with the oil situation, I can't see why it should be a problem. Just don't tell anyone where the picture came from for the time being. Apparently either the media or the National Security Administration, NSA, isn't being real open about what's going on here."

He printed off seven more copies and then emailed all of the Zs their own personalized copies along with the same warning. Couldn't forget Zandy and the boys.

***

Fourteen hours later, Damey finally gave it up for the night and crashed. He flopped down in bed, rolled over on his side, and shut his eyes.

Damey's mind once again turned to home. As he lay there tossing and turning, he thought of their first two week vacation of last summer. It had been one to remember. Week one was Washington DC and week two was the Appalachian Trail, just like they'd promised. The kids had been put in charge of the agenda, which made matters a bit complicated because they wanted to see and do everything. When kids have Mensa level IQ's, that's what happens.

Damey fell into a long, deep sleep, immediately returning to his dream state, picking up right where his mind had left off. "Okay, guys," Zandy said one night at the dinner table. "We've got to get a little realistic here. We're only spending one week in DC. There is no way we can visit one-hundred and eight places."

"But, Mom," Zaiden whined. "We cut the list way down. There are over two-hundred and fifty attractions there."

"We've never been there before," Zack said. "We've gotta see as much as possible. We just gotta"

"Yeah, who knows when we'll ever get there again," Zane said as he threw his arms in the air and squealed in a high-pitched voice. "You know what your boss does to most of our vacations."

Everyone laughed and looked right at Zack who wanted to crawl under the table. They would never let him live it down. That's OK, it worked.

On the day they left, Damey and Zandy had taken off work early on Friday, packed the SUV, and got as far as they could before stopping for the night. They arrived in DC in middle of the day Saturday. By the time they checked into their motel, it was too late to visit anything that would take a lot of time. To get themselves oriented, they drove by some of the monuments and sights they wanted to zero in on during the week.

The next morning, the kids wanted to go to the zoo first. Damey and Zandy figured three or four hours and they'd be off to the next place. When they left Monday night at eight-thirty, Damey said, "Enough. There are 2,000 animals in that place. We don't have to see all of them this time. Next time we come, we'll take over where we left off."

Not only did the boys want to see everything, but they had to read every word that was written about each and every exhibit. Same thing happened Tuesday at the Smithsonian National Air and Space Museum. There were four more "must sees" on the Smithsonian list.

"Dad, this isn't going to work," Zack said shaking his head. "One week isn't enough. There's too much to see and do."

"That's what Mom and I tried to tell you. You've got to cut down the list and quit spending so much time reading every single word printed about each and every exhibit."

"Uh huh," said Zandy. "Wonder where they got that from." She couldn't help but elbow Damey a little in the ribs.

"I'm not as bad as they are," he said pretending to be shocked, mortified, and indignant.

Their eyes met as they laughed.

One week later on Sunday morning they piled into the car and headed for Tennessee much to the chagrin of the Zs sitting in the back of the vehicle. They were excited about the hike, but way too few items had been eliminated from their DC list. They had to come back next year.

After four days on the trail, they were all ready to get off their feet. They caught a shuttle back to the car and headed cross country to Kentucky. Damey and Zandy surprised the kids with another day at Mammoth Cave. They'd been there on a three day weekend a couple of years previously, and the boys had pleaded for a return trip ever since. This time there were no interrupting phone calls. Then they drove home on Saturday giving them a day to rest up before going back to work on Monday. Damey and Zandy needed it. The kids started planning their August trip to Disney World.

CHAPTER 7

On the following day, the robot began to act like it was trying to follow a trail. It had quit veering off towards the left and right hand edges of the monitor. Damey gave Hector a couple of oral commands, programmed a few more directions with the keyboard, and waited.

Damey and the guardsmen on duty watched for a while half mesmerized by the back and forth jerky pattern it had been doing all morning. Suddenly, the robot straight-lined, acting like it had zeroed in on a target. "Go find Captain Morissy," Damey said to one of the onlookers. "I think we might be on to something."

Since there was nothing else he could do but wait at the moment, Damey called home again while waiting for Morissy to show. Nothing much had changed on the home front. Zandy and the kids were just a little more adamant, demanding to know how much longer this mission was going to take. Damey woefully admitted he had no clue. He did tell them, though, that maybe things were looking up. He'd have to let them know later. As it was, this one had to be a short call just to say "Hi" and that he was thinking of all of them.

By the time Morissy showed up, the robot had stopped. Damey turned on the lights and camera. After focusing the lens, what appeared to be an underwater oil well showed clearly. Ten feet off the surface they could all see the leak where a pipe just above the pump took a ninety degree turn and headed away from the device. Damey took pictures from several angles and printed them. They could be emailed or faxed whichever way the people in charge from the NSA in Washington wanted them.

The one thing they couldn't be sure of was whether or not it was an active, live, and pumping well. The hydraulic pistons didn't appear to be moving, but that didn't mean much. Maybe the rig only worked certain hours a day, week, or some other time period.

"Can you seal pipe and stop the leak?" Morissy asked.

"Yes, at least I think so," Damey said. "I can get started on that right away."

Using the hand controls on his computer that simulated the robot's claws, Damey moved the left claw to one of the legs on the rig. He clamped a hold of one of the supporting legs down near the bottom so the weight of the robot would not put any strain on the apparatus yet keep it steady and not moving while he worked on it. Not knowing if all the parts of the rig were rusted to a point of critical weakness gnawed at his mind. Everything would have to be done slowly and carefully.

Next he raised the extendable arm on the right claw ten feet off the surface so it was even with the spot where oil was oozing from the pipe. If the pipeline were new, he would be able to turn on the nuclear-powered laser, melt the steel he was using for solder, and seal the leak without causing any further damage. The problem was, he had no way of knowing the condition of the pipe spewing out the oil.

He decided to experiment. What he would do is melt some of the steel solder away from the leaking area and then turn off the flame. Before the icy water cooled it too much, he'd try to move the molten gob of steel to the pipe and paste it against the hole to see if it would stick. His first attempt failed because he missed the hole. However, the material did stick to the pipe and stay there without causing any apparent further damage.

On the third try, he actually hit the hole and slowed down the seepage. After several more repetitions, the leaking oil appeared to be stopped. It would take a few minutes until the ocean currents cleared the oil already in the water away from the rig until they could be sure. As the water cleared, it was apparent that he had accomplished the job, but he couldn't leave it that way. He had to make sure the molten steel weld would remain attached to the pipe. Carefully, he moved the laser closer to the seal. What he wanted to do was melt the gobs of steel into and around the hole without causing any more damage. If the laser hit the pipe directly, he was afraid he'd blow a hole in it that maybe could not be fixed.

It took six more hours before Damey felt satisfied the job was complete and secure. He ordered the robot to slowly circle the structure two more times just to make sure, and there were no signs of any further spillage. The next question was, could the pipeline coming out of the ground be sealed and the rig removed and brought up to the ship if the NSA wanted it done, without causing a catastrophic geyser that could not be sealed? The stress and strain on Damey had started to show.

Morissy checked in again and noticed. The guy needed to take a break. "Damey, it's nine p.m. and you've been glued to that seat since this morning. Before you do anything else, at bare minimum, you probably need a trip to the bathroom. Then, let's you and I go to the mess hall and grab a bite. We need to talk."

Damey stood up, yawned, stretched and motioned for the guardsmen controlling the icebreaker to come over. "I'm leaving the lights and monitor running so you men can keep an eye on things. If you see anything out of the ordinary happening, let us know immediately."

He pointed to where he'd sealed the pipe. "Pay particular attention to this area. Also, I think this other piece is the pump? Keep an eye on that area as well to see if anything changes. Right now, the device doesn't appear to be running. It's important to know if it starts. If it does, I think these things right here look like maybe they're pistons and will move up and down if the engine starts. If that happens, we'll know it's an active well." He used the computer's mouse as well as his finger against the monitor to make sure they understood the regions on the well he wanted them to keep track of.

He and Morissy went down to the officer's section of the cafeteria and ordered dinner. While they waited, both sipped a glass of dark blue grape wine and talked.

"If it is an active well, what do you want to do about it?" Damey asked.

"Depends on what that robot of yours is capable of doing. I know what I'd *like* to do. I'd like to shut it down, disassemble it, and bring it to the surface so we could maybe identify who it belongs to."

"Hector has a sister-robot we're using in the Oklahoma oil fields right now that can, not only find the best place to drill, but also partially erect an oil rig. Taking one down could be easily done with this one."

"Let's do it then."

"Not so fast. We need sanction from the authorities in Washington before we can do that. I won't do it without their sanction. "

"Yeah," Morissy said. "I don't want that one on my head either. I'll send out a coded message tonight with our findings so far. Don't want to tip off anyone monitoring us just in case. Then we'll see what they want to do.

After dinner, they checked back in top side. Nothing had changed—no more leaks and no sign of pump activity. Was it an active well? Was it one long ago abandoned after the underwater exploration and mining ban went into effect? There was no way to know for sure without dismantling the oil well and towing it to the surface.

In the meantime, Damey felt exhausted. He wanted to head down to his quarters and get some sleep. He wondered what Zandy and the kids were doing. They were eighteen hours behind them so it was around five in the morning. They'd better be sleeping.

***

Once again, Damey had no more than fallen to sleep when dreams of home and family returned. This time it was another early summer event.

"Boys, after breakfast get your lawns mowed right away. Mom's getting her hair done, and we're picking up Grandpa to get in a little hike at the mall. That'll give us old folks a little exercise, our massages, and then we'll all have lunch."

"But, Dad, it's gonna be really hot out there today. Can't we spend the day in the pool? You and Grandpa can go. We'll be okay," Zachary said.

"Wait a minute," Zaiden said. "It's my twelfth birthday on Monday. Do I get my first massage today or do I have to wait until next week?"

"I had planned on today, Zaid," Damey said. "However, if you three want to stay home and swim, maybe we can get Mr. Parkinson to come babysit."

"Dad, he's our lifeguard, not our babysitter," Zack grumbled.

"We gots to go with you and Grandpa then. I won't fall asleep like Zack always does."

"Not fair. I gotta wait a whole 'nother year before I get to get my first one," Zane whined. "'Sides, I bet you fall asleep half way through just like you-know-who. Instead of wasting that extra fifteen minutes Dad pays for, I should get it."

"Won't neither," Zaid said.

"You're not in the locker room at school; talk right for a change," Damey said giving them a little bit of a hard time. He and Zandy had to remind them once in a while to speak proper English around the old folks.

69

Damey and Zandy looked at each other and smiled, both thinking along the same lines. Their lives sure had changed in the past thirteen years. Three stair steps, each a year apart in age, and less than an inch in height, and all practically clones of their dad. People mixed the boys up all the time when they were by themselves—including their own parents.

Naturally Zandy denied it, but she did it more often than Damey. One day for fun, the kids sneaked a picture of twelve year-old Damey out of the album, and shuffled it in with their school pictures from last year. If it hadn't been for the difference in clothing, you wouldn't have been able to tell them apart. They looked like identical quads. They showed the collage to their parents, wanting to know which picture was a duplicate of one of them, and Damey smiled. He caught on right away. He remembered the shirt he'd worn on picture day that year. It was his favorite. Zandy was stupefied for a couple of seconds before she figured it out. They mounted and framed the group and hung it in the family room.

CHAPTER 8

The two guardsmen in control of the ship spent
more time watching Damey's monitor than what was
going on with the ship. Their number one duty was to
make sure the icebreaker did not become icebound. To
keep the water around the ship from freezing up, they
would move forward for five kilometers, roughly three
miles, and then put the ship in reverse and back it up.
Back and forth it went. Since they had put the engine on
autopilot, it would keep repeating the process on its
own. All they had to do was keep an eye on the controls
and look overboard periodically to check the ice
condition.

"Robot almost acts like it's freezing up. Hate to see
it get imbedded in the ice, and then not be able to do
anything," Sean, the senior guardsman said. "Wonder if
we should notify Dr. Williams?"

"Nah," responded Ivan, his shift partner. They were
good friends so the CO scheduled them as a duo.
"Williams says it stays warm because of the nuclear
battery. Why don't you tell Hector to snoop around on

the bottom to see if he can spot any more ancient sea critters? That'd keep him active."

"Do we dare?" Sean asked. "Williams says it only responds to his voice. Hate to have the thing go berserk on us down there." He laughed, visualizing the robot doing backflips.

"I don't think we could hurt it. Go ahead. You do it. You're the ranking dude here. That way if we screw something up, it's your fault," Ivan said.

"Thanks for all your heartwarming support. It would be kind of fun, though, to see if there is anything else down there lurking around."

Sean picked up the microphone and pushed the key. "Hector, wake up. Patrol the bottom for life forms."

"Did it twitch?" Ivan asked. "Looked like it moved. Try another command."

"Hector, search!" Sean said a little more emphatically.

Ivan even tried a couple of commands with no results. They tried another ten minutes or so and gave up. Hector simply would not respond to either one of their voices.

Three floors below them, Damey woke up, rolled over and looked at the clock. It was 4 a.m. He rolled back over thinking he should get up and go check on Hector. To hell with it. Everything's cool, he thought.

Cuddling up to his pillow, and unaware of any concerns on deck, he dozed off again.

Damey continued his dream where it had left off. Thinking about it later when he woke up, he thought it was strange he should dream about this event because it was just an incident that had been told to him by Andy Parkinson, their neighbor. After breakfast on that particular day, the kids had begun their lawn mowing detail. After each house on their to-do list, they traded implements so each one had a turn on the rider, the push mower, and the weed whacker. There were never any arguments or discussion, they just did it.

Andy and his wife lived in the house next door when Damey and Zandy moved in. Damey had started the mowing and shoveling routine then, and over time the boys took over the chore. Andy grumbled because Damey wouldn't take any money for it and wouldn't let him pay the boys either. Damey did relent a little and let him feed them hot cookies and lemonade. In the winter after they shoveled his sidewalk and driveway, he always asked them to come in when they finished for some hot chocolate along with their cookies.

On one occasion, Leo, Andy's cousin, had come for a visit on Friday and stayed the night. They stayed up late talking, as they hadn't connected in a few years, and both slept in. Andy got up first, put on the coffee, made a big pitcher of lemonade, and started his weekly baking chore.

In his dream, Damey saw Leo as he walked into the kitchen with a curious look on his face.

"Have a good night?" Andy asked as he pulled a hot tin of cookies out of the oven.

"Yeah, slept good. Ah, I love the smell of freshly baked chocolate chip cookies. Always do your baking this early in the morning?"

"Just on Saturdays. Have to get ready for my lawn mowing crew. They'll be here about nine."

"Got a lawn mowing service?"

"Kinda. The neighbor kids do it."

"Probably not too pricy then. Not like a regular service," Leo said as he checked out the cookies.

"Help yourself. There's plenty. Have to save out nine—each kid gets three plus lemonade. And, yes, they're pretty cheap. I'm not allowed to pay them. They mow the widow's to the south of them, their own, and mine. It's their 'community service' gig for the weekend."

"Cool. How'd that happen?"

"Their dad's idea. They're great neighbors, the whole family—mom, dad, and all three kids. Hope they never move. Their house doesn't really reflect their income. They should be living in some damned mansion. Oh well, grab the lemonade out of the fridge, will you? Let's go sit on the patio and watch. It's about that time," Andy said as he grabbed the platter of

exactly nine cookies and three glasses filled with ice cubes.

They set the treats on a side table, covered them with a paper towel to keep the flies off, and sat down.

That's them over there doing their yard. They always start with their other neighbor's yard and work this way. I'm last on the agenda. Probably should complain."

"Yeah, right. Noisy little critters, aren't they?" Leo said.

"Just laughing and having fun. You should hear them in the afternoon when they're in the pool. Nothing but squeals, laughter, and splashes. There's playful competition to determine who did the best cannon ball, who really won the race, and did so-and-so really get clobbered with the beach ball or did it miss. They're a rip.

"It's totally different, though, when their dad isn't around," Andy continued. "About every other month or so, Dewline sends Damey on some big 'emergency' to fix somebody else's problem. When they do, the kids go into a funk and you don't see or hear much of them. They absolutely hate it when he's gone.

"You should hear them when they start ranting about it to me. I'm not sure what they say, if anything, about the situation at home to their mom. But, I sure do get an earful when he's gone. They whine that it's totally unfair because there are at least another

hundred engineers or so who could do the job, but since he's the best, he's the one who gets sent. The oldest kid actually wishes his dad would quit his job and go out to MSU and head up their robotics department—a job that apparently is a standing offer. Can you imagine the pay cut he'd take for doing that? Hell, the kids wouldn't care. At least their dad would be home all the time then."

Leo looked out over the yard as the threesome moved toward them. When they hit the property line, the kids stopped, switched whichever apparatus they were using, and continued with their chore. At this point, the oldest one drove the rider, the middle one navigated the push mower, and the youngest handled the weed whacker. "How long before they spot the cookies?"

"I'm sure they already have, but with you here, I'll have to stop the process and call them over while the cookies are still warm." Andy stood up, whistled to get their attention, and waved his arm towards himself so they'd come over.

Zack, the boy on the rider, shook his head and right hand in a, 'No, that's okay' motion and mouthed, 'You've got company,' and kept mowing while watching out of the corner of his eye.

Andy waved his arms over the top of his head in a crisscrossing fashion to get their attention, scowled, and pointed down at his foot in an up and down motion.

All three devices stopped in place, and the boys walked to the patio grinning as they eyeballed the platter.

"We didn't want to interrupt when you had company, Mr. Parkinson," Zack said.

"Right. Like I bought these out for the flies. Boys, I want you to meet my cousin, Leo Parkinson. Leo, this is Zachary, Zaiden, and Zane."

All three firmly shook hands with Leo and told him they were pleased to meet him.

"Sit down, pour your lemonade, and get those cookies while they're still warm," Andy said.

They did, and then the conversation became much more animated and lively than Leo was used to. There were times when he had trouble keeping track because it seemed like everyone talked at the same time. Andy noticed his head as it bounced from boy to boy looking confused.

"What's the matter, Leo, having trouble keeping up?" Andy asked. Then he laughed. "They talk non-stop and fast. Ya gotta focus, man."

About that time Damey came over to the edge of his yard and called out to the boys. "Guys, Mr. Parkinson has company. You shouldn't be over there butting in. Get your work done and come home."

"Damey, they're fine. Come on over and meet my cousin from Indianapolis."

Damey walked across the grass with a big smile on his face, stuck out his hand to Leo when he made it to the patio, and said, "Hi, I'm Damey."

"Damey, this is my cousin Leo. Leo, I want you to meet Dr. Damarian Williams, vice president in charge of robotics at Dewline Engineering and father of this part of the Z-Team."

"Glad to meet you, Dr. Williams."

"It's Damey, and it's a pleasure to meet you too, Leo."

Damey looked over at the empty tray, opened his eyes wide, and said, "You piglets scarfed down all the cookies and didn't even save one for your poor old dad?"

Looking guilty, all three offered him one of their own they had clutched securely in their fists.

"You know I'm just picking on you," Damey said smiling. "Enjoy and then get your jobs done. As soon as you finish and clean up, we're going to pick up Grandpa. If you want to get in any pool time later, you'd better get hustling."

"Damey, I've got more cookies in the house. Let me go grab some." Andy said.

"Oh, good grief, no," Damey said waving his hand. "I don't want any. You know I have to hassle the rug rats or they'd think something was wrong."

Damey stayed and chatted for a few minutes as the boy's finished Andy's lawn. Then he had to go. Zaid's first massage at the mall was waiting.

CHAPTER 9

When Damey woke up in the morning, he crawled out of bed, did his morning routine, and headed topside. He checked the monitor and nothing had changed. The seal on the pipe appeared to be holding. All of those same old questions went through his mind. How long had that apparatus been there? Was everything so corroded because of the salt water, that tampering with it might cause another major leak they couldn't fix? Was it really a relatively new, active well that some renegade country or oil company had installed? Could he or Dewline be personally held accountable for creating some international incident? They weren't going to know anything for sure unless they sealed the well permanently, cut the legs off the oil well, and brought the entire rig it to the surface and loaded it on board where it could be shipped off to the government laboratories in Washington DC.

Damey stared at the screen, pondering the situation. Out of the corner of his eye, he saw movement. He looked up and saw Captain Morissy walking towards him. "Any word from Washington?"

"Not a word," Morissy said. "Seems like we ought to hear something soon, though. They're usually pretty prompt—especially on important stuff. I'm betting we hear something this morning. Can't forget the fifteen hour time difference."

"I know. It took my body two days to adjust," Damey said. "Hard to believe it's still yesterday at home. Almost kind of futuristic."

Damey looked at his watch. "Weird, isn't it? Right now it's eleven a.m. on the nineteenth of October here, and seven p.m. on the eighteenth there. Oh well, if they made a decision yesterday, we should get word on it pretty quickly 'cause, according to my figures, they shut down for the day a couple of hours ago. Which reminds me, it's time to call Zandy and the kids."

Damey walked out of the cabin into the sub-zero degree temperatures. That's where he would get the best satellite reception for his call. He punched in Zandy's number.

Thirty minutes later, he walked back into the cabin. His mind was still ruminating on the call. As usual, the kids weren't handling his absence well at all. He hardly understood a thing Zack said through his tears. He was going to have to get home soon.

Captain Morissy met him inside with a printed document in his hand. With a big smile on his face,

Morissy handed the document to Damey. "Read this. Time to find out if that toy of yours can really do the job."

The government had authorized them to seal the well, dismantle the rig, and haul it aboard if at all possible. The unknown, invisible, authorities from the NSA back in Washington who make these kinds of decisions wanted it sent stateside in order to identify the origin of the oil well and determine if it is a current rig or some old abandoned, non-operating relic from the days before the international agreement made in the 80s like they suspected.

Sifting through the legal and political jargon, the message was clear. As soon as they had it on board, the oil rig would be air lifted via helicopter to McMurdo Station and then flown by military transport to some secret government research facility in the D.C. area for inspection. Damey and his robot would then be flown on a separate plane straight back to Michigan.

"Guess we'd better get to work," Damey said. "Hope all the working parts on the robot keep operating as well in that frigid salt water as they did when we sealed the well. It's been sitting there idle for a while, so knock on wood. At least everything's worked fine so far. Let's just hope our good luck continues."

"So, what's the process? How do you plan to actually do it?"

"That's where my computer and all of its special properties come in. I will be running the operation from here just as if I were sitting in a car seat on the back of the robot. The best way I can describe it is that it's sort of like one of those flight simulators used to train pilots. The only difference is, instead of the device flying through videos, or whatever it is they use, I'll be controlling the robot from several miles away. What makes it a little awkward is there will be a few seconds time delay."

"I thought your robot had a brain of its own so all you had to do was tell it to do something, and it would," Morissy said with a slightly sarcastic edge to his voice.

"That only goes so far. The sensing, seeking, and discovery part was pretty much done that way. Now that we've found it, I have to operate certain parts by hand. It's a safety technological measure for now. For instance, we wouldn't want the robot to be able to go looking for the well, find it, and then disable and seal it or spring an even bigger leak all on its own without direction from a controller."

"Personally, I don't think you can dismantle that well without having an uncontrollable gusher of oil. You understand, don't you, I advised against this part of the operation. I just wanted to seal the leak if you could and leave it."

"I know," Damey said. "But, I guess we all have our bosses. If my kids had their way, I wouldn't even be here."

His conversation with his family was still fresh enough in his mind that he didn't need any of Morissy's ego trips. Besides, that isn't what he said earlier, Damey thought to himself. He wanted to dismantle it and bring the rig on board as well. Now he's suddenly covering his ass in case something goes wrong?

Without another word, Damey pushed the button that cranked up the juice to his main control station. As he manipulated buttons, the giant monitor moved so that it centered itself right in front of them. The screen with all the programming language slid off to the side and out of the way.

About fifteen minutes later, Damey, talking mostly to the guardsmen standing around watching, said, "These two handles control Hector's claws. Watch the time delay as I move this right one towards that right leg of the rig."

Damey stood up, leaned forward, and pointed to what he was talking about on the screen. Then he moved the handle forward and slightly to the right. Slowly the robot's hand moved towards one of the steel legs supporting the oil rig. After several minutes of maneuvering, Damey clamped the jaws of the robotic hand shut taking a firm grip on that piece of equipment.

Next he'd have to extend the left arm to the other side of the rig so he could center the robot between the legs for better balance. Within two hours, Damey had the apparatus below centered and secured in the grasp of the robot. A wand-like device was able to move away from the body of the robot and sever the remaining legs with the nuclear powered laser. He did not cut the legs held by the robot. He didn't want the rig to start shifting around by itself and ripping away from the main oil line—leaving them a blinding oil gusher to deal with. He could visualize the sneer on Morissy's face if that happened.

"OK, here's where it gets tricky. I've designed the robot to be able to burn a half inch gap through that pipe. While it's working its way through the pipe, a quarter inch thick molten sheet of steel will immediately follow, sealing the pipe as I cut through it. There will obviously be some oil spillage, but we should be okay."

"Suppose it doesn't work?" Morissy asked.

"Then we'll have a twenty inch pipe uncontrollably gushing oil into the Weddell Sea."

"Don't even say that."

Damey tilted his head upwards to Captain Morissy. "Ready?"

Morissy raised his eyebrows, shrugged his shoulders and nodded. What else could he do but pray that the robot did its job?

85

Without even waiting for a verbal answer, Damey refocused his attention on the screen in front of him and started pushing buttons. They could see the laser arm slowly move to the middle of the pipe. Damey pushed a button and the laser beam shot forward. From hundreds of feet away they could see sparks and splinters of steel on the monitor as the beam started its cut through the pipe moving slowly from left to right. They could see small signs of seepage but nothing disastrous—yet. The biggest concern was they couldn't tell for sure how well the replacement cap was sealing the pipe. The oil that did escape clouded their vision.

After another hour, Damey said, "There! We're completely through the pipe. If the oil stops leaking, we'll know how well it worked. Don't be surprised if we need to reseal a couple of the edges. That molten steel might have cooled off too quickly in that frigid water to create a perfect seal the first time.

They waited a while and just watched. Gradually the water cleared. There were two small areas that needed to be redone, and then the leaking stopped for good.

Just to be sure, Damey took an extra hour and ran an added layer of molten steel around the new lid.

Morissy watched without commenting a whole lot. He didn't want to distract Damey any more than he had to at this point. He'd never admit it, but what he had just witnessed awed him.

Damey stood up and stretched. "Step one completed, Captain. Now, on to step two."

"What now? All you've got to do is cut those last two legs and drag the rig back to the ship, right?"

"Not quite," Damey said. "This pipe coming off the main rig to the right here transporting the oil to who-knows-where should be sealed as well. That way we're not taking a chance of it leaking thousands of gallons of oil back into the water. If there isn't a pump working on the other end, whatever oil is in the pipe would automatically flow back out of the opening. Haven't seen anything to know one way or the other, but I guess I don't want to either.

"If we knew for sure that there was a pump at the other end pulling the oil their way, it might be more fun to leave the gaping pipe and let them suck in a ton of sea water before they could shut down the operation on their end. I don't think we can take that chance."

"You're in charge, Dr. Williams," Morissy said. "Do whatever you think makes the most sense."

"This operation will take longer. The pipe's covered with sea mud making it harder to see what we're doing. Also the cut-and-seal operation will be vertical instead of horizontal. Haven't ever tried it that way before." Which was a lie. Damey had tested the device in every position possible, but he wanted to make the captain sweat a little more. Morissy had turned into such a jerk, he deserved a little more stress. Damey so wanted to look up and see Morissy's expression, but he didn't. He forced himself to stare at the monitor instead.

CHAPTER 10

Within two hours the pipe designed to deliver the oil to its destination had been severed and double-sealed. Damey stood up and stretched, then pressed both fists into his sides as he arched his back. "Cafeteria's still open isn't it?"

"Yep. Open twenty-four-seven. Let's go get a bite to eat."

"Sounds good to me," Damey said. When we get back, I'll double check all the seals one more time, and then we'll cut those last two legs holding the rig steady and start hauling the thing in. Might take a few hours once it starts. Also, I think I want to attach the cable as well before we start towing it towards the ship, instead of relying only on the robot's claws. No sense using nothing but the claws to hold on to the rig when we have a backup so handy. Don't want to put any more strain on Hector's hands than we have to. If they broke loose, I don't know what would happen. It'd probably disable the damned robot, and then we'd lose it and the oil rig."

"Dr. Williams, I wish you'd quit telling me all of these potential horror scenarios. I'd like to get a little sleep tonight as well."

"Call me Damey, and I'll try to oblige," he said with a grin.

For the first time since Damey'd been there, Morissy smiled, not only with his mouth, but also with his eyes as they shook hands.

After making their way through the cafeteria line, they sat down at a table together and relaxed.

"So, tell me. What do your wife and kids think about this big adventure you're on? I'm sure the kids are seeing it as exciting even if your wife isn't," Morissy said.

"Zandy has been treating it as a normal business trip just like always. She's getting sick of these excursions too. There are a number of other people around there who could do them, but Sam, our owner, always wants me to do them, 'Just to make sure they're done right.' Anyway, she's the steadying force behind the whole family when it comes to these trips.

" The kids hate it when I'm gone and are completely paranoid and irritable. I think they've Googled every possible bad thing that could happen in the Antarctica and are convinced that we are going to experience every one of them. My thirteen-year-old blubbered through our whole conversation this morning. I don't even know what he said."

"He's the oldest, right? I think you said they're all a year apart. They're right at that emotional stage," Morissy said.

"Tell me about it," Damey said. "I'll be so glad when they get through puberty. My mom and dad laugh about it. They keep telling me I'm just getting well-deserved paybacks. Personally, I don't remember being all that emotional as a kid."

Damey and Captain Morissy talked for about an hour, mostly about family and friends. Not much was said about the job at hand. The captain was leaving that all up to Damey anyway. By the time they went back up to the chow line to pick out a piece of pie, their relationship had finally evolved into a friendship. The sarcastic digs and distrust by Morissy had disappeared. He acted as if he enjoyed talking to Damey. When their conversation did switch to the robot, he didn't understand half of what Damey told him, but he appreciated and liked the results so far.

After their break, they walked back into the cabin. When they got to the front of the robot's computer, one of the guardsmen approached the Captain. "Sir, McMurdo's notified us a few minutes ago that we're under a severe storm warning tonight. They hadn't said anything before because they thought the front was going north of us. It shifted suddenly, and we're going to have high, gusty winds, heavy snows, ice shifts, etc.

They said the sea would be rolling under us so currents and waves might get pretty rough."

"Okay, thanks for the warning," Morissy said. He looked over at Damey. "Think you can get that rig cut loose and start hauling it towards the ship right away? We get these warnings periodically. Sometimes they aren't nearly as bad as forecast, sometimes worse. Never know for sure until it gets here. The forecasters have a horrible time getting it right down here on the bottom of the world for some reason or the other."

"I think we'd better. I'd been half tempted to wait until morning so I'd be a little fresher and more with it mentally, but I think the adrenalin's pumping after listening to the news. Let's get it done. By the way, how bad does the ship rock in one of these storms? Any Dramamine handy?"

"Oh, it's never that bad. The icebreaker isn't all that huge so it does jump around a bit, but you'll be asleep by the time it hits, and you'll never even notice it."

"Hope not."

Within the next hour, the robot's cable had been attached to the top of oil rig and the last two legs holding the well severed. With luck, it didn't move. Moving slowly, trying not to disturb the rig in any way which was standing precariously on its four unattached legs, Damey raised the robot to a position of twenty or so feet above. That's as far as the claw arms would extend. Then he reeled in the cable so there was equal pressure among the claws and cable. Damey's plan was that with a simultaneous steady pull upwards with the robot's cable and claws would enable the rig to rise upwards instead of falling over into the mud.

That's where it required more guesswork on Damey's part. How much force did he dare use, pulling with the cable? He needed the robot's arms and the cable to work in sync enough to keep it from falling and dragging along the ocean floor, but not so much that he took a chance of snapping anything. This time, he didn't relay his concerns to the captain.

When he was ready, he turned to Morissy and said, "Keep your eyes on the rig now, it should lift right off the deck standing upright. Once we have liftoff, I'll stop things for just a minute to make sure everything is stable, and then up we go."

Everything worked smoothly, and the robot and rig commenced its journey back to the ship. Damey estimated about a three-hour time period. Exhaustion crept in.

"All we can do now is watch the monitor and wait. You don't need me right now, so I'm going to bed. I've programmed it so when the robot pops to the surface, it should be right off the port side of the ship. When it does, push this button right here on the computer. That will disengage the claws. The cable is strong enough to keep the oil well from sinking. Then grab the robot with the crane, haul it on board, and secure it tightly so the weight of the oil well doesn't drag it overboard. The lead to the oil well is only about twenty feet, so it's going to be right there. Have a bunch of the guardsmen handy to grab a hold of the cable, play a little game of tug-of-war, and haul it aboard. At that point, don't worry about standing it up or anything. Drag it up on its side and secure it so that it doesn't slide back off. Nothing I can do unless the robot stops working. If it does, come and get me. If not, get it done, and let me sleep."

***

Down in his quarters, Damey crawled into bed. His nerves were wound so tightly, there was no way he could sleep, exhausted physically as he was. He found the only way he could truly relax was to forget the robot and oil well and think about home and family. As he tried to make himself comfortable in the bed, their annual Fourth of July party popped into his mind.

Damey viewed himself off to the side of the pool deck watching eighteen of his nephews, nieces, and other various relatives playing water volleyball in the shallow end of the pool. After eating, they had to stay out of the deep water for an hour—no diving or cannonballs. Surprisingly, the kids' game had already lasted two hours and was still going strong.

They never kept score and cheered for the other team when somebody made a good shot or save. The object was to have fun, not to win.

"Uncle Damey," Layla, one of his four nieces said. She and a couple of other girls were taking a break from the game. After they rested up and got their breaths back, they'd return and join up with whichever team was short handed.

"What, Honey?"

"How do they do it? Where do they put it?"

"What are you talking about?"

"When Aunt Zandy yelled that dinner was ready, all the boys charged to the head of the line so I just stood back and watched," Layla said. "For starters, how big were those hamburgers? They were huge."

"Oh, I had them made up special. They were half pound ground sirloin patties," Damey said.

"No wonder they looked so big. Anyway, I stood back and watched Zack fill his plate. He started with that huge cheeseburger on an oversized bun, stacked on tomato, onion, lettuce, pickles, and then smeared the top bun with salad dressing and hot mustard. I swear it stood four inches high. No way could it fit into his mouth. He had to nibble around the edges.

"Then he filled up his plate with baked beans, potato salad, and that yogurt-based fruit salad to the point that it was spilling over the sides before he got his lemonade and sat down. Then, to top it off, he went

*back for seconds to get another burger and more beans.
How? I watched. All the other boys did the same thing.
It made me half sick. Why aren't they all fat? If I ate the
way they do, I'd weigh three-hundred pounds."*

"You know, Layla, there's an old cliché that goes
something like this, 'Girls eat to live, but boys live to
eat.' Does that make any sense to you?"

"Yeah, I get it. Makes perfect sense. Every boy I
know does love to eat."

"Yeah, that's the way I look at it too. Besides, the
Zs are in the pool for hours every day in the summer.
That's how they stay skinny. How many calories do you
think they've burned off today all ready?"

"No clue. All I know is that I can't keep up with any
of them. Did you see them when I did my first
cannonball? I had fifteen boys all lecturing me on the
correct form so I could create an 'appropriate' splash.
Then a bunch of them demonstrated the right
'technique' before making me practice my jumps to
their satisfaction. I swear. They're all nuts."

"Won't argue with you on that one either," Damey
said laughing. "But, those boys do burn a ton of energy
out there in the pool, and I don't know if you've
noticed, there's also a continuous flow towards the
bathroom."

"I know. I had to stand in line when I went in
there."

"Mom!" Zaid hollered after he'd stopped the game and waved his arms over his head, staring at his mother, trying to get her attention.

"OK, OK, I know, it's pie time," Zandy said. "But you guys are responsible for setting up dessert. We need the six pies on the counter, bowls, spoons, a spatula, the ice cream scoop, and the frozen vanilla yogurt in the freezer all brought out here and set on the table."

"Oh, my God, no," Layla said as the boys all jumped out of the pool, toweled off quickly, and headed for the house. "How could they?"

Damey had no answer. He laughed.

With a smile on his face, Damey lay in bed and felt very comfortable. He was relaxing and starting to get sleepy. It wouldn't be long, and he would be out. That's when his memory picked up again.

At eight-thirty that evening, he watched Zandy hold up one finger. By eight-forty-five, Zack's IPad had slipped out of his hands and she held up the third. Within fifteen minutes, all three boys had slumped over in their chairs and fallen asleep.

At nine-thirty, Zandy went over to Zane and shook him awake enough to put his footrest down and shoo him off to bed. At nine-forty-five, she repeated the process with Zaid, and at ten with Zack. All three managed to brush their teeth, strip, and fall into their beds without cleaning up or pajamas. They'd spent the better part of six hours that day in the pool, so they didn't need showers.

Damey and Zandy covered them with their blankets when they did their nightly routine of tucking them in and kissing them goodnight. The only one ever vaguely aware that they did it every night was Zack, but not that night. Like his brothers, he was out like a filament-fried light bulb.

"It's a good thing we're understanding parents and don't wake them up and make them go to bed when they fall asleep an hour before bedtime," Zandy said with a fake serious look on her face.

"How right you are," Damey said with a frown. "It's not 'fair to punish them by sending them to bed just because they're 'resting their eyes.' The fact they're half snoring with their mouths open because they're half sitting and halfway tipped over in horribly uncomfortable positions is completely irrelevant."

"Glad to see you understand that," Zandy said.

CHAPTER 11

"Whoa, it's getting rough," Morissy said as he held on to the hand rail. The words were barely out of his mouth when the ship lurched to the left, leaving everyone with the sensation that the vessel had almost tipped onto its side.

The winds blew gustier and stronger as the warm front neared. The guardsmen on deck hoped that with luck the temperature might even edge up above zero. That'd be different. Snow blanketed the skies and visibility dropped to zero in whiteout conditions. The fifty mile per hour winds rocked the ship making it bounce off the floating icebergs. Ivan and Sean, the seamen watching the computer screens, fastened their seat belts even though they were safely tucked away in the control tower. Normally, they didn't bother. Everyone else on duty went below deck to lower levels. People had been blown overboard during storms like this and were never seen again.

"You hear what I just heard?" Ivan asked.

"Thunder! Joy, joy. What next?" said Sean. "Never thought we'd get it here."

"Thunder snow is rare all over the globe, but it does happen," Ivan said. "Check with the weather station at McMurdo and see how much of this we're supposed to get."

A few minutes later, Sean returned. "According to them, the snow's dumping at a rate of four inches per hour. They don't know for sure how long it's going to continue. They just kept repeating that it's all because of the warm front. It doesn't sound to me like they know what the hell's going on. He also repeated about every other sentence that there isn't much we can do but wait it out.

"Hopefully the damned robot will continue making its way to the surface with the oil rig still attached. That'd be all we need right now is to lose it because of the storm. It's bad enough knowing that when it does surface, there's no way we can try to bring it all aboard until the weather settles down."

Flash! Crack! A lightning bolt pierced the window of the cabin and hit the steel protective backing of the main computer running the ship. Both crew members instinctively tried to dive for cover, but were strapped into their seats. Everything around them went quiet and dark. Fortunately the electrical charge didn't touch the seamen cowering behind Damey's computer.

They both fumbled with shaky hands as they unhooked their seatbelts. Standing on wobbly legs, they looked at the main computer.

"Don't touch it," Ivan said. "It might still have an electrical charge. I'm not interested in getting myself electrocuted right now.

"I've got a rubber-handled screwdriver in my tool box," Sean said. "Hold on a minute. I'll run and grab it."

Two minutes later he was back. He tapped the two dead computers and Damey's live one in several places. No sparks.

"Let's try rebooting both of them. Hopefully, the lightning didn't do anything other than turn them off, and they'll be OK," Ivan said.

They pushed the *Start* button on both computers. Nothing happened. Why? They were hooked to Williams' nuclear-powered computer. It's not like they were connected to the ship's power.

***

Unaware of the storm and the havoc it had caused, Damey was still lying in bed reliving the Fourth of July pool party from the previous summer in his mind. It was his way of relaxing and getting his mind off the robot and oil rig they were pulling to the ship. Finally, he drifted off to sleep. The rocking of the ship hadn't fazed him yet. As he had fallen asleep with home and family on his mind, it was only natural for his dreams to carry on with what he'd been thinking about. The dream, however, began on a late Saturday afternoon in the second week of July.

Damey and Zandy were relaxing in the living room, reading the day's newspaper as the kids frolicked in the pool. That's when the doorbell rang. Damey looked over at Zandy with that, "Now what?" expression on his face as he pushed himself out of his chair, and answered the door.

"Registered letter for Dr. Damarian Williams," The postman said.

"Yeah, that's me. A registered letter? What do we have here?"

"Sign here. It's something from a lawyer's office in Lawton, Oklahoma. Must be important. Overnighted from a little after twelve noon yesterday. Cost 'um a bundle."

Damey scribbled his name on the dotted line and then stood there as the mailman headed back to his truck. His mind whirled. Lawton, Oklahoma? He hadn't thought of the place in ages. That was Xavier's home town. What gives?

The irony involved with the loves of his life's names all sounding so much like the person he despised the most in the world burst into his brain—Xavier. There

*was that "Z" sounding connection between Zandy and
Xavier—Zack and Xavier—Zaid and Xavier—Zane and
Xavier. He hadn't thought of it in years. How weird
was that? He wouldn't change a thing.*

*"What's going on, Honey? Don't just stand there
with the door open," Zandy said.*

*Damey turned around and walked a little unsteadily
back into the living room and sat down. He tossed the
envelope to Zandy.*

"What's this?" she asked.

"Don't know. Don't want to know. You look at it."

*Zandy picked it up and glanced at the packet. The
return address read 'Baker and Bannerman, PC,'
Lawton, Oklahoma. Damey had told her about Xavier
when they'd first started dating, but it had never even
been a topic of conversation since. It was just
something that had happened a long, long time ago and
he wanted to forget it.*

*She, however, hadn't forgotten it. At the time she'd
thought it was strange, because even though she
occasionally tried to bring the subject up, he would
never talk about the guy or what had happened when he
and his mother had gone out to Oklahoma. One time
she built up the courage to ask Ty what was going on.
He shrugged his shoulders and told her she'd have to
ask Damey. She never did again. Whatever had
happened, it was obvious he didn't want to talk about it*

so she'd let it drop. As she looked at the envelope, those conversations of years ago popped into her head.

She looked over at Damey. He sat rigidly, staring straight ahead. She looked at her watch. The boys would be playing in the pool for at least another hour or so—she hoped. Then they'd come charging in starving and looking for their dinners. She didn't want them to see their father looking like he was in complete shock. Whatever! Damey had to open the envelope.

"Honey, you can't just sit there staring off into space. Open the letter. It must be important if they spent all that money to ship it overnight delivery. Here."

"No. You open it," Damey Said. "I don't think I even want to know what it says."

"You're not even acting like yourself. Nothing ever fazes you. I've never seen you so shook up. Just because it's the town where your biological father lives, doesn't mean it's about him."

"He's not my father. He was the sperm donor. My father and the kids' only grandfather on my side of the family is Tyrone Williams."

"All right. Settle down. I'll look." Shaking her head, Zandy tore open the envelope and pulled out the set of documents. There was a cover letter and a will. Scanning the cover letter, she muttered something unintelligible under her breath.

Completely unaware of the more violent rocking of the ship and the fact that there was no electricity, heat, power, running water, or anything else working on the ship, Damey slept on. The two guardsmen topside were fighting the elements in a panic mode as Damey dreamed on facing a panic situation of his own.

"So, what does it say?" Damey asked.

"Well, the quick version is, Xavier Rufus Armstrong passed away earlier this summer and has been cremated. His ashes were disposed of by the crematorium, according to Mr. Armstrong's last wishes. Per his instructions, the house and all belongings were sold at public auction as soon as possible after his death. Sounds like he'd been sick for quite a while and had this all arranged in advance As you are the sole heir and beneficiary of the will, you need to show up in person with proper identification to collect what is left after fees, taxes, estate settlement, miscellaneous bills, etc."

"I don't want his damned money," Damey said. "We don't need it. I couldn't spend it. I won't take it."

"Not that simple, Honey. If you don't go out there and collect it, the money will just get tied up in some trust fund and sit there forever, or, at least until the lawyer's fees shrink the account to zero. You have to do something with it. If there is enough so it would be worthwhile, you could always set up some kind of

scholarship fund for college kids or maybe donate it to the schools to set up a permanently funded robotics club, give it to the park system or something like that. Just because you think he's worthless, doesn't mean his money can't do some good for somebody."

"How sardonic would that be? We could call it the, 'Xavier Rufus Armstrong Scholarship Fund.' Bull! I wouldn't honor him with something like that," Damey said.

"Quit being a jerk just because you hate him. Think about it. Whatever the total amounts to, it could be given anonymously to some local charity, and hopefully be very helpful for some needy people in the town."

"Does it say what we're supposed to do?"

"Ah, wait a minute. Yeah, down here on the bottom. Everything is ready for your signature and collection of proceeds. They're hoping you can make an appearance before the last week of July. That's when the law firm's shutting down for vacation. He's asking you to call his secretary and set up an appointment," Zandy said. "Since you have to make a personal appearance to sign for the check, let's make a quickie week's vacation out of it. There must be something we could do out there with the kids for a day or two."

"OK, on Monday will you call the lawyer and find out how much money we're talking about? If there's enough, tell him we want to set up a college scholarship fund for disadvantaged youth. Maybe he can take care

of that too, and we can fax documents and signatures. I don't want to go out there. The only way I'd do it is if I could see Mary and Tom in Okmulgee and Ella in Lawton. I doubt if either place is still in business. What's it been, twenty-five, twenty-six years? No way. Those Mom and Pop type places never stay open that many years. Nope, they'd be impossible to find."

"Who are those people? I've never heard them mentioned before."

"Mary and Tom owned the motel I stayed at while I waited for Grandpa and Dad to come and get me. They essentially took care of me and fed me for a couple of days. They were fantastic people. Ella was the girl who worked in the restaurant in Lawton. Her parents owned the place. In the week I was there, we became friends. She even printed off a map for me to ride my bike to Lansing."

"We'll put our Google genius boys on the job to see if either of those establishments still exist and who might possibly be the owners," Zandy said. "Maybe they'd know how to find your friends. All we can do is give it a try."

CHAPTER 12

Ivan and Sean looked at each other, wondering what they should do. Neither one really had a clue. It was scary, and they were alone. Most everyone else onboard was asleep.

"Try a light switch, Ivan. See if they will go back on by flicking it up and down.

"Nope. No electricity. Wonderful. Is the engine still running? I don't hear anything. Try backing up and see what happens."

"Nothing," Sean said. "Engine's dead. We're stuck here in the ice. I hope the heat's still working. Feel anything from the air duct?"

"We're getting nothing, not even cold air. The electricity must be out over the entire ship. This place is going to get nasty in a hurry."

"Let's check and see if the robot's doing anything," Sean said. That should be running on its own power."

They walked over to the side of the ship and looked. They saw nothing but ice forming, leading up to the side of the ship in an area that had been ice free earlier. Between moving the ship back and forth and the turban engine vibrations, they'd been able to keep a significant ice free zone for when the robot and oil well surfaced. That area had already started to close. It wouldn't be long and they'd be icebound again.

"We better go get Morissy," Ivan said. "This doesn't look good at all. Why don't you go get him? I'll stay here and keep playing with the controls to see if I can get anything to start back up. Might as well try rebooting the computers again while I'm at it."

OK, but it's still thundering and lightning out there. Better watch and make sure I don't touch anything metal," Sean said.

"Why? You know that lightning never hits the same place twice,"

"Bull! That's nothing but an old myth."

"Probably. Doesn't matter. Just go get him. Besides, ever stop to think? The whole damned ship is steel. That's what we're standing on," Ivan said.

"Thanks. That did wonders for my stress level," Sean said smiling. Being the one to have to go wake up Morissy didn't exactly thrill him.

***

Damey was still oblivious of the problems Sean and Ivan were facing topside. The mental and physical fatigue kept him in a deep slumber in spite of the rocking and tumbling of the ship.

109

As he continued to sleep and dream of home, the earlier smile on his face turned to a frown. Having to go to Oklahoma to sign off on his biological father's inheritance was neither a wanted nor welcome journey. Would the boys want to go? Would they get angry and rebel? Would Zack sneak into Sam's office and raise hell again?

In his dream, events unfolded later that afternoon when the boys got out of the pool and came in declaring their starvation. Zandy told them to grab an apple out of the fruit bowl. Dinner would be a little later than usual.

Then, Damey sat the three boys down on the sofa and explained the ancient history regarding Xavier, Ella, and Lawton, Oklahoma. He also told them about Mary and Tom putting him up in their motel in Okmulgee until his Grandpa Berkeley and Ty could get out there and pick him up.

" Stop! Stop! Wait!" Zack snarled. "Two things. Are you trying to tell us that Grandpa isn't our real grandpa? I don't believe that. No way!"

"Whoa! Hold on," Damey said. "Remember what I just told you? Grandpa adopted me, so, yes, he is my father and your grandpa. Even if he hadn't adopted me, he'd still be your grandpa. Could any grandpa on Earth love you more than Grandpa Williams?"

"No."

"Then, what's the issue? I've told you before, pure biological relationships don't always mean much. The only relationships that are important are the human ones. Look at all your aunts, uncles, and cousins. You aren't biologically related to any of them. Does that matter? Look at another example on your mom's side. Who are you closer to, Aunt Mimi or Uncle Robby?"

"Aunt Mimi. She always spoils us," Zack said.

"Which one is your mom's actual sibling?" Damey said.

"Okay, I get it. But there's still the second thing. What about our vacation to Disney Land in August?" Zack said.

"Maybe that's on hold for this year. After all, Mom and I don't get the whole summer off like you guys. Why don't we plan on it next year?"

"Not fair," Zack said. "We've been planning on our trip for a long time now."

By that time all three boys were complaining loudly at the same time with expressions to match their tones.

Zaiden slapped his hand on his knee. "Screwed again. You and Mom's 'posed to get four weeks of vacation this summer. This year was gonna be different. Now we're only gonna get two after Mr. Wardwell promised four, 'cause Dewline's always too busy." He stretched out the word 'busy' to sound like it ended with twenty Zs. "Why don't you quit that place and get a

*regular job like teaching robotics out at MSU or
something cool like that?"*

*"I know it isn't fair to you guys. You had Disney
World all planned, but let's have fun with what we
have. To start with, we have a research project for you.
Hopefully, it will all end up as something different and
fun. Of course, if you don't want to take a road trip,
another alternative is the four of you staying here while
I take a plane and fly out by myself. Of course, then
maybe we wouldn't get another family vacation of any
kind this summer."*

*That sold the boys on the Oklahoma trip. Hyped up
with the challenge, Zack, Zaid, and Zane went to work
while Zandy started dinner.*

*While the boys did their research, Damey said,
"Zandy, I've got to crawl up into the attic and see if I
can find a package stashed in my old storage chest up
there. Be right back"*

*Zandy shrugged her shoulders. She had no idea
what he was talking about. All she knew that there was
a chest up there with some of his childhood "treasures"
that he said he wanted to share with the boys when the
time was right.*

*He made it back to the living room with a packet
just about the same time the boys came up from the
family room with their news. They already had the
results. Much to Damey's surprise, both businesses
were still in operation with Mary and Tom listed as*

owners and operators of the motel and Ella named as owner of Ella's Place.

That's when he showed Zandy and the boys his old map. "Ella put this together for me to ride a bike on the back roads from Oklahoma to Michigan. For some unknown reason, I never disposed of this package of maps covering the route. Since she was my first girlfriend, I wonder if I didn't because she wrote her name on the front of the big manila envelope."

"You were going to ride your bike from Oklahoma to Michigan?" Zane asked. "Dad, were you nuts?"

"No comment," Damey answered smiling.

That, too, turned into a quick exercise for the boys. They discovered that all those roads still existed. The boys, just like their dad, much preferred the back roads over the super highways. Staring at the highway, cars, and trucks for hours at a time bored all of them. They much preferred looking at cows, horses, fields, wildlife, woods, and little towns.

"Why don't we fly and rent a car while we're there?" Zandy asked. "It'd be a lot quicker and we'd have more time to do some things there."

The boys quickly vetoed that idea. Following Ella's map sounded like a lot more fun. Not only that, but it reminded them of food again. It was time for dinner.

Monday morning Damey and Zandy went in and sat down with Sam, their boss and owner of Dewline. They knew it wasn't going to be pretty. He'd set up everyone's vacation and work schedules for the summer planning on the two of them being gone the last couple weeks in August, not July.

Sam rocked back in his chair and looked at both of them before speaking. "While you're there, what do you think about stopping by some of those oil producers and showing them the design of what you've been working on? That automated oil-sniffing robot's about ready, right? All those companies have wells out in the Atlantic. I'm sure you could convince them that they all HAD to have one of them for deep water inspections, leaks, and repair. I bet there are other uses for that thing we've never thought of."

"You're probably right, but I don't think it's quite ready yet. However, we could certainly present them with the idea," Damey said.

"Yeah, why not? We have that little model robot you've been playing with. We could throw it in the back of the SUV and take it along for 'Show and Tell,'" Zandy said as they all kind of looked at each other.

Sam smiled. If they pulled this off with some success, it'd be one hell of a break for the company. "Well, spend the rest of the week seeing how close you can get it to being operational. If everyone works on it, you should be able to pull it off. Shouldn't be that big a deal, should it? Why don't you guys slip out of here around noon on Friday? That'll maybe give you a

*couple of extra days to present the concept to some of
those oil execs and see what they think of the idea?"*

*"Don't know why we couldn't," Damey said as he
looked at Zandy who just kind of shrugged her
shoulders and raised her eyebrows.*

*"Okay, I'll have one of the secretaries start making
some contacts and see if she can line up some potential
meetings with oil execs around the Lawton area. That
way we can cross the whole thing off as a business trip.
Think positive, you two. All of us will be able to write it
off on our income taxes this way. You know what? I'll
bet marine biologists and the military could find uses
for that thing too."*

*The three of them stood, smiled, and shook hands.
"Thanks, Sam. It's going to be another adventure for
the boys—and, oh yeah, don't spend all your time
thinking up future trips for me while we're gone."*

Ivan held on to Damey's robot's mechanized hands
to keep his balance while Sean went to go get Morissy
out of bed. "I can't believe he's sleeping through this
storm," he said aloud even though no one was around to
hear him.

Ivan looked around as the sweat beaded on his
forehead. His mind went wild with anxiety. *Will the
damned ship turn over? Should we go to everyone's
sleeping quarters and get everybody out of bed? Should
we ready the lifeboats? Where the hell is Morissy?*

115

Ivan walked over to the side of the ship again to see if he could see the robot or oil rig, holding on to anything available. Nothing. All he saw was one wave after another splashing against the side of the icebreaker and a layer of ice forming on its side.

If the ice gets too thick, we'll sink like a rock and nobody will ever know what happened to us or where our bodies are, Ivan thought. *Maybe it'd be better not to wake everyone. They'll all drown in their sleep and nobody will ever know the difference. Nobody, that is, except me and Sean and maybe Morissy if he ever gets his dumb ass up.*

He made his way back to the controls and tried the communications system again. Nothing worked except Damey's nuclear powered computer, and that hummed away like absolutely nothing was wrong.

Ivan couldn't take it any longer. He screamed at the top of his lungs, "MORISSY WHERE ARE YOU?"

Three levels below, Damey still lay curled up and sound asleep, unaware of the condition of the ship and the danger everyone was in. His dream, regarding last summer's trip to Oklahoma where he had to wrap up legal issues dealing with his biological father's estate and make some business calls to oil executives to promote his new oil-sniffing robot, continued.

Damey visualized the scene as it evolved at the house a few days before they were ready to go. He sat the kids down again to explain a last minute stunt he'd come up with as Zandy watched and listened. She hadn't heard of this twist either. "All three of you poor souls look exactly like me. Zack, since you're the same age I was when that fiasco in Oklahoma happened years ago, so you're going to be the guinea pig. We're going to stop at the motel and try to pull a fast one over on Mary and Tom in Okmulgee, and then we'll try it again on Ella when we get to Lawton."

"What?" Zack said. "What are you getting me into?" He smiled that impish grin of his, knowing his dad's sense of humor.

"Nothing bad. This should be fun. Here's what I have in mind…"

The family left Lansing right after lunch at their favorite neighborhood restaurant on Friday afternoon. They would spend two nights on the road and get into Okmulgee relatively early Sunday morning, planning to spend the whole day there and that night.

Around ten o'clock on Sunday morning, Zack walked into the motel sporting a gigantic smile. "Good morning, Sir. I just talked to my grandpa in Michigan on the phone from that gas station down the street, and after his throwing a fit about my latest stunt, he told me about this place and said I should come in here and ask if you'd call him back and set it up so I could stay in one of your rooms until he can get here to pick me up."

117

"Oh, my," the man behind the counter said as his voice trailed off. He paused for just a moment and turned his head to the open door behind him. "Mary, would you come in here a minute, please? I want you to look at this young man. He just now walked in the door and wants us to call his grandpa in Michigan to see if he can stay here for a day or so until somebody comes and gets him."

Mary ambled into the office wiping her hands on a towel. She'd been doing the laundry on her first load from early check-outs and had washed her hands after handling the soiled sheets. She took one look and dropped the towel on the floor. Her jaw dropped. "Little Damey," she whispered.

"That's what my grandpa calls me when I'm trying to pull a fast one on somebody. My name is really Zachary Williams, but I go by Zack."

"Williams?" Tom said. "Isn't that what the man's last name was who came along with the boy's Grandpa?"

"Yes, I think so. What was his first name, something like Theron or Ted or something like that?" Mary said.

"Would it be more like Tyrone or Ty?" Zack asked with his face splitting so wide open it showed every tooth in his mouth. "That's my grandpa's name. My dad's name is Damey."

"*Zack, where is your daddy? I want to know, NOW.*" *Mary said. She grasped both of his shoulders with her hands and stared into his eyes.*

"*My best guess is that he, Mom, and my brothers are standing outside of the door laughing their heads off.*"

"*Damey, get in here. I want to see you,*" *Mary shouted as she gave Zack a quick hug.*

Damey, Zandy, Zaiden, and Zane walked in together laughing. They shared hugs even before introductions.

After names were given, Mary asked, "Identical triplets?"

"*Line up,*" *Damey said as the boys shuffled into a row on cue like they'd done many times before so Mary and Tom could see the fraction of an inch difference in height between each of them. "Nope, they're stair steps, almost exactly a year apart. Zachary, Zaiden, and Zane in that order.*"

"*Yeah, after they finally got the product perfected, they quit,*" *Zane said with a straight face.*

He pretended to be insulted when they all laughed at him but couldn't pull it off. He laughed too.

They spent the day at the pool and with Tom and Mary as much as business allowed. Monday morning they planned to drive on to Lawton and hole up there until they finished the financial business of Xavier's will and their meetings with the oil executives.

119

Taking a break from the sun, Damey and Zandy came back into the office just to chat alone with Tom and Mary.

"This next week's not going to be that great for the kids, but I'm sure they'll find something to do besides playing games on their iPads." Zandy said during the course of their conversation.

"Why don't you leave them here?" Mary said. "They seem to be great kids and would probably spend all their time in the pool if today is any indication."

"They would. They love our pool at home, but I can't expect you to watch after them. Besides, they have to eat. And, oh boy, can they eat," Damey said. "Besides, I want them to meet Ella who printed off the map for me."

"You still have that same old envelope full of maps you followed on your bike from Lawton?" Tom asked. "That's wild. I still think of that pile of maps every once in a while and shake my head. I figured you either had a lot of guts or were a little loco. Maybe when the boys come in from the pool, I can run that by them."

Damey laughed. "Yep. We followed the route she planned all the way out here from Michigan, and we're going to follow my bike route from here to Lawton. But, no, don't ask the kids if their old man is crazy. They'd agree way too quickly and hurt my feelings."

When new motel customers came in, either Damey or Zandy would slip out and check up on the boys.

When Zandy did, she'd slather them again with the sunscreen she'd borrowed from Mary just to make sure.

"I can understand you wanting them to meet Ella," Mary said during one of their interludes, "but if Lawton is going to take more than a day or so, bring them back. We'd be happy to look after them for however long it takes. From the sounds of things, you're going to be busy so the boys will just be hanging around by themselves anyway. Might as well be here playing in the pool. Besides, no kid could eat as much as you did those couple or three days we had you, so you can't use that for an excuse."

Right at that moment, the three Zs walked in on their way to a bathroom break and heard that last comment. All of them laughed uproariously claiming genetics and making numerous comments about their dad's appetite as Damey shook his head and rolled his eyes—like each of them would have done if the tables were turned.

CHAPTER 13

Damey's dream had been going on for several hours without the ship's rocking bothering him. As the turbulence became more severe, he woke, but wasn't concerned. The guardsmen had told him there was going to be a storm. He thought to himself, *no big deal.* Then he heard and felt the ship slam against the ice shield, floating icebergs, or something. He didn't know for sure what the ship was hitting. The only thing he was sure of was that he knew it was bouncing off of something. He sat up and looked around. It was totally black in there. Then the ship bounced again. Whatever it was hitting made the ship rock back and forth multiple times. It didn't act like it wanted to quit.

Damey felt turmoil rising in his stomach. He knew that feeling meant he was going to get sick so he headed blindly for the bathroom. There were no lights, but he knew the general direction he needed to go and managed to find it before his stomach erupted. As soon as he did, he shoved his head into the toilet. The results

122

were not pleasant. Satisfied that the episode was finally over, he stood. Looking around and seeing nothing but blackness, he started feeling his way back to bed, hoping that it wouldn't happen again. His tasty dinner was no longer with him. Oh, well, he thought to himself. Things should be better in the morning, and he'd certainly be ready to get something to eat again then. He'd survive, he thought to himself as he smiled. No way would he even try to eat again right away.

He wondered why it was so dark in there. He hadn't remembered it being so pitch dark before. Not even the light on the clock showed. Then he remembered. Earlier, he had heard a loud *"Crack,"* and then a snapping sound at the door. That's when the lights went out. He figured that somehow the rocking and bouncing of the ship had caused a fuse to blow in his quarters. It hadn't bothered him at the time because he knew that in the morning one of the guardsmen would know where the breakers were, and he'd take care of fixing it.

Now, however, things were different. After heaving his guts, he was wide awake. It took a while, but he finally made it from the bathroom back to the bed. That took a lot longer than it had when his stomach was churning. Feeling around the bed, he found his clothes, and put them on. He thought maybe he should go topside to see what was going on and check the progress on the robot while he was there and tell somebody about his lights.

Using his hands as guides, he moved to the end of the bed which had been placed against the wall and then slowly started following it to the left. As he moved around the room towards the door, he bumped into a few things, but he didn't hurt himself or knock anything over so he continued. As he felt his way along, he thought about what it must be like to be blind in an unfamiliar place. That would be tough. After what seemed like forever, he found the door and grabbed the handle. The doorknob turned, but the door didn't budge.

Then he remembered that he'd slipped the slide bolt shut. He ran his hand up the door until he found it and slid the bolt to the right. Home free, he thought to himself. He turned the doorknob again and pulled. Nothing. Somehow, that steel door had secured itself to the wall like it had been welded shut. He couldn't even wiggle it. Then he remembered what Morissy had said about the security locks. Was that a safety feature of some kind connected to his blown fuse? Now what?

As he stood there wondering what he was going to do, he became aware of the terrible taste in his mouth. He hadn't rinsed it with water or mouthwash after getting sick, and the aftertaste was almost as bad as the original nausea attack. He decided to make his way around the wall again and find the bathroom. The least he could do was flush out the sour taste while he waited to be rescued.

When he finally found the lavatory, he turned on the faucet. Nothing. No lights, no water, nada. Wonderful! He wrinkled his nose as he realized he hadn't flushed the toilet after getting sick. He didn't dare do it then and waste the water in the tank. Hopefully, that supply of water wouldn't drain out of the container until he had to use it. In the meantime, he lifted the top and splashed fresh water in his mouth. He swished it around, gargled a little, and spit it into the toilet. He hated doing it because he didn't want to waste whatever water he had on mere vomit.

He found his way back to the bed and lay down. The ship was still rocking, but not nearly as badly as it had been earlier. He pulled out his cell phone and looked at the time. It was four AM. Knowing that it wouldn't work, he punched one on the phone anyway. That was Zandy's speed dial. He listened. Nothing. He punched the off button and decided not to waste his battery. At least he could keep track of the time. He wondered how long it would take for them to realize he was locked in and get him out of there. As he lay there, he shut his eyes and eventually drowsed off again. For some unknown reason, his dream picked up right where it had left off.

***

The next morning, Damey and the Z-Team headed down the lonely road he'd used while riding Xavier's bike into town those many years previously. This time it was in reverse. The gas station where he'd stopped to make the call to Grandpa was no longer there. He pointed out the spot to Zandy and the boys. It had been replaced by a mini-mall. As they rode along, Damey kept looking out the window on his side of the car. About an hour after they left town, he whipped over to the side of the road and stopped.

"I want to check something out." He felt really weird inside. He knew he must have a strange expression on his face as well because they were all staring at him. He couldn't help how he appeared, and he wasn't talking about what was really on his mind.

Without another word, Damey got out of the car, crossed the road, and walked towards a little stand of trees, maybe one-hundred feet off the road. The other four followed looking at each other and shrugging their shoulders but not talking. He could feel them watching him.

Inside the first couple of rows of trees, they found a little clearing. He looked around at the setting and then lifted his head towards the top of the trees. High above the ground he saw the frayed remnants of a rope hanging from a limb. He stared uttering not a word. The others followed his gaze.

Zandy put her arm around Damey's waist and gave him a reassuring squeeze. Whatever was going on in that head of his, he needed to know he wasn't alone. She'd find out about the rope when the boys weren't around.

"Looks almost like a good place to camp out.," she said trying to refocus the group. "Did you spend one of your nights here?"

"Yes, I did," Damey said with a sudden smile on his face. "Leaned the bike against that tree and then curled up on the ground right here in the middle. They were having one of those late summer cold spells, and I darned near froze to death. Brrrr! I still remember my teeth chattering before I fell asleep. I'm sure it wasn't all that cold, but I wasn't dressed for sleeping on the grass wearing a short-sleeved shirt.

"When I left here the next morning, it took me until probably close to four o'clock before I hit Okmulgee."

"That long? What a slow poke," Zane said. "We've only been gone about an hour."

"Figure it out," Damey said. "We've been driving around fifty miles an hour on this old road, and as sore as my legs were from the day before, I'd have been lucky to be going seven or eight."

CHAPTER 14

Ten minutes later, Morissy showed up with Ivan looking like he had just been dragged out of bed—hair uncombed, a five-o'clock shadow, and shoes untied.

"What the hell happened?" He asked stifling a yawn.

"Lightning knocked out the main computer. Don't know if Dr. Williams' computer is damaged or not. At least it seems to be running—probably because of the nuclear power setup he has. Looks like our backup is dead in the water too. We tried rebooting both of them and nothing happened," Ivan said.

"Better check the engine room and see if anything shorted out. Are the engines even running?"

"Don't think so," Sean said. "We aren't getting heat either. I don't think anything is running."

"That's all we need," Morissy mumbled. "Still don't know why we got stuck on this oil leak chase. It's been one pain in the ass after another. Speaking of pains, before you make that engine room inspection, maybe you'd better go get Williams. Hopefully he didn't fall out of bed and hurt himself. Besides, maybe he'll know what to do."

Ivan grabbed the biggest lantern he could find and the two of them groped and stumbled down three flights of stairs through the darkness towards Damey's room.

Holding the lantern in his right hand, he alternately pointed it at the floor where they were walking and then back to the wall trying to spot the door. They'd forgotten how isolated that room was from the rest of the ship. It was in an area where they never went.

With the light shining on the wall and straight ahead, Ivan didn't see an item that had fallen off the shelving unit. He stumbled over it and landed flat on his face, knocking the wind out of him. The lantern skittered twenty feet ahead of him. Normally, an item that small would never have made him lose his balance, but the surprise factor got him. During the turmoil, Sean tripped over Ivan so they both ended up in a heap on the floor.

They lay on the floor a minute trying to catch their breaths. Panic started to set in. "Where's the light?" Sean asked.

"It's gotta be here someplace," Ivan said. "Stay down and see if we can find it. With luck, it just turned itself off."

They flattened themselves on the floor moving their hands and arms back and forth trying to find the light. They hoped it hadn't broken when it skidded across the floor. It shouldn't have. After all, their lanterns were built to take a lot of punishment. More by accident than anything else, they found it. The lens and bulb had both been shattered by a doorstop sticking up from the floor. Sean picked it up, tried the switch just to make sure, and then threw it across the room uttering a number of obscenities in the process. When the lantern hit the wall, it burst into pieces.

Totally in the dark, they continued to crawl on their hands and knees towards what they hoped would lead them to the wall again. Then maybe they could follow it to the door that closed off the nose of the ship from the rest of the vessel where Dr. Williams was located. Unlike the spaces between the various sections on the first two levels which were always open, because of air circulation, heating, and air conditioning, all the sections on the lower decks had sealed doors, none of which were ever left open. With no light filtering into the area, it made navigation all the harder. If they could get their bearings once they found the wall, hopefully they could find Williams' quarters.

Neither Sean nor Ivan was familiar with the third deck because their quarters and the officer's lounges were all located on the second deck. Their work area was topside. Neither had been on this floor more than once or twice in the six months they'd been on the icebreaker which meant all their movements were pretty much guesswork.

They crept towards the wall feeling like a blind baby exploring his new playpen for the first time. Once they made it, they weren't sure if they should stand up or continue to crawl so they wouldn't trip over something else. They kept crawling, keeping their bodies in contact with the wall until their knees started hurting. Then they stood up and crept along, keeping their shoulders in contact with the wall as they moved their hands back and forth hoping not to run into anything. Finally, they found what they hoped was Damey's door. Much to their chagrin, it was locked. Both pounded on the door and yelled.

"Dr. Williams, can you hear us?"

Finally, after several minutes, they heard pounding from the other side of the wall.

"Can you unlock the slide bolt in the door?" Sean yelled.

"Slide your hand up and down the frame and then try to unlock it," Ivan shouted.

They heard a faint response from inside. "Something else is holding it shut. I already undid the slide bolt."

"Crap! It's the ship's safety locks. They've backfired. Williams is locked in like a prisoner," Sean said. Then he yelled through the crack in the door, "We'll be back. Might have to break down the door."

They worked their way back to the passageway leading to the second deck. Opening it, the brightness from the sunlight filtering down felt like needles stabbing their eyes. Blinking and rubbing them, they made their way topside with Sean going one way and Ivan the other.

"Why didn't we think to prop open the doors when we went down there?" Sean asked.

"I don't know. Stupid I guess. They closed themselves behind us, and we had the lantern. Never even thought of it," Ivan said.

When they got back on deck, they found Morissy standing there staring blankly at the computers. He shook his head, wondering what more could go wrong.

Then he found out as Ivan broke the news. "The lights are out over the entire ship, and Dr. Williams' door is bolted shut with the jail locks. Our bolting system worked in reverse when we lost power. Instead of unlocking the security deadbolts, the damned thing locked him in.

"Where's Sean?" Morissy asked.

"He headed to the tool room to see if he could find a power saw or cutting torch to break open the door."

"Let's go take a look and see if he's found anything."

Making their way through the darkness with their lanterns, they met Sean on his way back.

"Those doors are locked too since they're connected to the same circuit as the brig. Can't get in," Sean said. "Somehow we've got to get a hold of some computer geek and get this mess straightened out."

"Yeah, how sweet is it that our own is on paternity leave. That freaking kid of his had to decide to come a month early. Don't we have someone else on board who knows anything about these damned computers?"

"Not really. We've got a bunch of gamers and hacks, but with all the personnel rotation lately, he's the only one left who's really a programmer and knows what's going on the inside of a computer. His only real backup was that guy you didn't like so you had him transferred. Who knows where he is now. There aren't any other ships within helicopter distance either because of the secrecy of this damned oil well mission we're on. The Feds are intentionally keeping everyone else out of this area so not to draw any suspicion."

"What about McMurdo? Are our communication systems working so we can call for help from them or one of the other ships which are probably all still a thousand miles away?"

"No, Ivan said. All communications are shut down. All we have are cell phones."

"I can't call anyone on another ship. I don't have numbers for them. I'll go out on the deck where we get the best reception and call the Department of Defense inWashington. In the meantime, see if you can find a fire axe or something. We've got to try to break down Williams' door," Morissy said.

"I do have a friend over at McMurdo," Sean said. "I'll call him and see if they have any computer geeks or hackers who would be knowledgeable enough to help. Doubtful though, good ones are kind of few and far between. While I'm at it, I'll ask him to report what we have going on to his CO. Maybe he can contact the DOD as well. We need all the help we can get."

Morissy made his way back topside. The wind was still blowing at a steady forty miles per hour, and the snow swirled. He went into the computer room first where they could sometimes get a satellite signal so they could call and sometimes not. It didn't work.

He went outside and tried again from the deck. He connected.

After explaining his predicament, the response was typical. They'd pass-the-buck and notify the computer gurus and turn the problem over to them. Someone would get back to him. Great! Did they expect him to stand out on the deck in the middle of a thunder blizzard and wait to hear back? Right! He'd check with the crew to see if they'd had any luck.

"Captain Morissy, Captain Morissy, we've got a problem," one of the ship's ensigns yelled as he ran up to Morissy all out of breath.

"What now?" Morissy asked not really wanting to know.

"There's smoke seeping out of Engine Room Two. Smells electrical. Don't know for sure. We haven't opened the door 'cause we don't want to feed it with oxygen just in case. Wanted to contact you first."

"How could it be electrical? We don't have any juice on this rig."

"No clue. That's just what it smells like."

"Round up everyone you can with flashlights and fire extinguishers and let's go check it out. That's all we need."

CHAPTER 15

Wide awake and wondering what would happen next, Damey made his way back to bed. Hopefully, those guardsmen would figure out a way to get him out of there. He stretched. All he'd done, for who knows how long, was lie in bed and sleep. At least most of the time his dreams had kept him entertained thinking about home and his and Zandy's adventures with the kids.

Somehow or the other, he had to get in some exercise. He didn't want all of his muscles and internal organs to atrophy as he lay curled up in bed doing nothing for days on end. With his leg brushing against the side of the bed, Damey did ten or so squats. He didn't count them because he was paying too much attention to his stiffness. He began to wonder how long he'd actually been locked in his room. It didn't seem like it had been that long, but who knew? It was almost impossible to keep track of time. He looked at his cell phone. According to the date on that, he'd been there for two days.

He wondered if he could walk in place for a couple of hours. Maybe by that time, somebody would figure out how to get him out. Fifteen minutes after he started, he checked the time again. This wasn't going to work. He had to think of another way.

Maybe if he could reenact his dream cycle, he'd be able to keep walking and not think about the stiffness in his legs. He let his mind wander to where his last dream had left off. They had spent a day and night with Mary and Tom at the motel in Okmulgee before heading on to Lawton. He and his family had just stopped at the campground where he'd spent his last night those twenty-six years previously before contacting Grandpa Tutor. His memory picked up the scene after he and the Zs left the campground.

He smiled as he watched himself and his family pull into Lawton and park a little ways down the block from Ella's Place. He was sure she wouldn't look out the window and recognize him after all those years, but he didn't want to take a chance. He wanted to give their scam a chance. After they walked by to double check and make sure she was in there, Zack, according to their prearranged plans, armed with the package of maps strolled into the restaurant. He made his way up to the counter unnoticed because Ella was writing the day's lunch specials on the chalk board and hadn't seen or heard him.

"Excuse me, Ms. Ella, but I have a question," Zack said.

Ella turned around and looked. The first thing she saw was that face—a face out of her past. She slapped herself on the chest and gasped. "Oh my God, you almost gave me a heart attack."

"I'm not that scary to look at, am I?" Zack laughed, unable to keep the straight face he'd practiced.

"No, not at all. It's just that you look exactly like somebody I knew years and years ago—long before you were ever born. I'm sorry, but you really threw me off guard. You said you had a question."

"Yes, Ma'am. A couple of weeks ago I was at home rummaging through the attic and found this old pack of maps with the name, Ella, written here on the outside of the envelope." He held up the package and showed her. "Didn't recognize the handwriting and didn't know where it came from, so I jumped on my bike and followed the route. It took me days to get here, but it finally brought me to your restaurant. Who are you, and why am I here?"

"You lie! Where is your daddy? I want to see him, now," Ella said. She clapped her hands together and giggled like the teenager she'd been the last time she'd seen Damey.

Laughing, Damey and the the Z-Team walked into the restaurant. After hugs all around and introductions, they all sat down to a soft drink.

"Remember, boys. No straws. Ella will think you're a real wuss if you do."

"Damey, that's okay. They can drink out of straws if that's what they're used to. I don't care. I guess I outgrew that one."

"I didn't. I've never used a straw since I left this place. They don't either. I brung 'um up good, Ella."

After the kids laughed at their dad's slaughtering of the King's English, he told her why they were there. He wanted them to meet her, but he'd probably have Zandy run them back to Okmulgee in the morning. The couple at the motel had offered to take care of them, and the Zs wanted to stay there because of the pool.

Besides, he knew he and Zandy would be tied up with the lawyers and business meetings for who knew how long, and the boys would be on their own. None of them wanted that. So, he'd rent a car for the next day and try to polish off the will details while she was gone. She needed to be back when they met with the oil reps. Then the two of them would work as a team explaining their new robot and its functions.

After lunch and a lot of catching up with Ella, the group went for a little ride around town. Before looking for a motel, Damey wanted to drive by Xavier's old place. He stopped out in front and tried to describe to the boys what it had looked like back then. It didn't really matter, because the lot sat there as empty as Damey's feelings in the pit of his stomach. The house had been bulldozed and nothing remained but a grassy field. Good, he thought to himself.

Since there was some kind of oil producer's convention going on in town, rooms were at a premium. The first couple of places they checked had no vacancies. On their third try, they found one.

"You have three children?" the desk clerk asked. "This is a higher class facility than most, and we try to keep things quiet and peaceful around here."

"Oh, that's OK. We make sure they stop racing up and down the halls screaming at the top of their lungs by at least two a.m.," Damey snarled with a penetrating glare and tone to his voice the boys only heard when they'd leaped way over that metaphorical behavior line drawn in the sand.

Zandy and the boys all made eye contact with wide-open eyes and raised brows. Speaking like that to a total stranger was way out of character for Damey. The boys took a step back as Zandy slipped her arm around his waist.

"Oh, I'm sorry. Really, I am. I didn't mean to offend. I just wanted to suggest that we have a number of older guests who tend to go to bed early." The clerk's face reddened as he slid the registration form over for Damey to sign.

He hoped the guest would accept his apology and not report him. He'd be fired on the spot for that comment. He didn't even know why he'd said it. Probably 'cause he just plain didn't like kids.

Damey started to fill out the form. "Zack, go check and see what our license plate number is, would you, please? I can never remember the darned thing."

"Sure, Dad," Zack said as he raced out the door. He would have liked to head back to Okmulgee that afternoon. He wanted out of there. He knew when he wasn't wanted.

After they got their luggage into the room, Damey couldn't help but wonder if the town was jinxed. Is Ella the only person in this town worth anything? Can't be. He'd only met three people from the place, and two of them were jerks. Lousy odds. Oh, well. They'd get the kids back to Tom and Mary's the next day. They'd have to. This so-called high class joint didn't even have a pool. How would the kids ever survive that?

As they settled into their adjoining rooms, the boys talked softly among themselves about what they'd just witnessed. They were bored out of their minds, but they didn't plan to say or do a thing. Their dad still acted a little out of sorts. They turned on the TV to see if there was anything worth watching. There wasn't. They pulled out their Kindles and iPads. They could always find something to do on them.

In the mean time, Damey called the lawyer to confirm his appointment. Then he looked over his scheduled meetings with the various oil producers the secretary had set up for him and Zandy. With the convention in town, they might be able to contact a few others as well.

Zandy stood up with her hands on her hips and sighed. "We're not going to see the boys for almost four whole days. Are we going to all sit around in our rooms and be miserable for the rest of the day?"

"No, let's take them to a park some place so they can get out and run around a little and burn off some energy. Later we can go out to dinner, and then what do you think about a movie?" Damey said

"Works for me. Let's get their grouchy old dad into a little better mood." Zandy said.

All three of the Zs smiled in silent agreement.

***

On deck it was a flurry of activity. Smoke had been detected coming out of the engine room. Within minutes a number of trained guardsmen were dressed in their firefighting paraphernalia and self-contained breathing equipment. Their group consisted of crewmen from all over the ship—cooks, engineers, ship operators, and a bevy of other personnel. Before moving, Petty Officer Patrick Mayhew checked each person's equipment visually making sure all zippers were zipped and all seals sealed.

Mayhew faced the crew, pointed to his bright yellow sleeves to remind them he was the team leader and to keep an eye on him. With everyone carrying fire extinguishers and lanterns, he led them into the darkness. Morissy, dressed like everyone else, followed behind. There wasn't anything he could do but get in the way, but he still wanted to be there. It was his ship.

Once they'd stumbled their ways down the steps and made it to the engine room, Mayhew spoke again. "Stand back a little but have your fire extinguishers ready. When I open this door, oxygen will feed any flames and we might get a burst of fire. Here goes."

When he opened the door, nothing happened except for the accumulated smoke billowing out the door. With what could almost be described as a group sigh of relief, the only hot spot they found was a trash can smoldered in the corner containing some wires leading off the engine beside it. It took less than thirty seconds to drench the thing and quell the smoke.

"What do you think happened?"

"Look at this lead. When the lightning surged through the ship's system, it must have burst from this frayed wire and into the metal trash can grounding out the charge. When we get power back, we'll have to replace this thing," Mayhew said. "In the meantime, we need to tie these wires off and let them dangle in the air without touching anything. We need to keep them from causing any more problems when we get electricity again. Then, we'd better inspect every room down here for any other troubles we might have overlooked."

No other damage or areas of concern were found. Hard to say who was more relieved—Captain Morissy, Petty Officer Mayhew, or the crew who would have had to fight an engine or structural fire with lanterns and fire extinguishers.

Leaving the door propped open so the room could air out, everyone hustled topside to get out of the hot, cumbersome, sweaty gear.

CHAPTER 16

Totally unaware of the drama going on around him, Damey continued walking in place trying to keep the blood flowing in his body. After that, he did some pushups, situps, and other exercises. He had to do something physical to pass the time.

For no better reason than to keep his mind off the ship's problems that he could do nothing about, he continued reliving the trip to Oklahoma with his family the summer before. At least they'd had a reasonably enjoyable evening their first night in Lawton, regardless of how things started at the motel.

Before Zandy headed down the road with the kids to take them back to Tom and Mary's Motel, the five of them had breakfast together filled with laughter, anticipation, and fun. The boys were ready for a change of scenery and the pool.

Damey hadn't actually witnessed the next part of their adventure, but he'd been told about it enough so he had the picture in his mind.

"Hi, Mary. We're back," Zack said as the three
boys trooped into the motel ahead of their mother
around eleven.

Normally, the kids would never be allowed to call
adults by their first names, but Tom and Mary had
insisted. In fact, Damey had never heard their last
names until the boys had checked them out on Google
when they did their research.

"You save our room for us?" Zane asked.

"You're all set, guys," Mary said. "Here's your
key. Pool's waiting for you, but no skinny dipping. Put
your suits on first."

The three of them stopped dead in their tracks,
turned, and looked at her mischievous smile. Everybody
laughed as they bolted for the door dragging their
luggage.

Zandy held up her hand and shouted to get their
attention, "After you get your suits on, stop by here
before you get in the water. I'm going to be leaving
shortly, and I want a hugs and kisses from the three of
you before I pull out while you're still dry and not
dripping water all over me."

They waved at her over their shoulders and raced
out the door. She didn't know if it had sunk in or not.
Didn't matter. She wouldn't leave without saying
goodbye to them anyway. Three to four days without
them would seem like forever. They'd never been
separated that long. Even the STEM camps the boys

*went to every summer at MSU were day camps. They
came home every night for dinner and bed.*

*As soon as they were out the door, Zandy turned to
Mary. "I need to give you some grocery money." She
pulled six fifties out of her purse and handed them to
her. "Keep track, and I'll catch up the extra I owe you
when we get back. I'm guessing it will be Friday
sometime. Hopefully, it'll be early in the day. The kids
aren't used to us being apart. They might get
homesick."*

*"I don't need all this money. They don't eat that
much."*

*"Oh, yes they do. Like Damey says, behind their
backs of course, 'It's a steady flow—in one end and out
the other.' Quick warning—if you take them to the store
with you, your bill will automatically inflate by fifty."*

"They spot and want all the good junk-food?"

*"No, for the most part, they eat none of that. I never
buy any or have it in the house. It's just that they seem
to find all these things that we NEED and can't live
without."*

*Mary laughed. Then she said, "Oh, another thing.
Tom and I talked about it and decided we'd keep them
with us during the day when they aren't in the pool.
We'll only have them spend time in their rooms alone
when it's time for them to go to bed. Somehow, I can't
visualize that group wanting to sit around a motel room
doing nothing but watching TV anyway. I've got all*

kinds of games and things here for them to do if they get
tired of swimming. I also have tons of sunscreen and
will keep them plastered with that."

"Oh, great! I'd forgotten about that. They take
care of putting sunscreen on each other at home all the
time, so I didn't even to think about it—much less bring
some."

"Not a problem. People leave that stuff here all the
time. Oh, and speaking of bed times, when are they?"

"Zane heads to the showers at 9:30, Zaid 9:45, and
Zack at 10. They're real good about it too. They're so
active during the day, they're exhausted by then. In
fact, Zack falls asleep in his chair most nights around
nine-thirty. And, of course, you realize, it would be
'NOT FAIR' to send him to bed earlier just because
he's 'resting his eyes.'"

Shortly, the boys showed back up in the office with
suits on and towels thrown over their shoulders. Before
Zandy left, Mary had the whole group go into her and
Tom's apartment so she could show them around and
explain the ground rules.

"There's the bathroom over there. When you need
to use it, don't bother going back to your room, just slip
in there. Look over in this drawer. You'll see probably
twenty tubes of sunscreen in here people have left pool
side. Lather each other up now before you go out.

"Make sure you use this multiple times a day. I
don't want to hear a bunch of crying and whining about

sunburn. In the meantime, I think we ought to have lunch before you go out. It's been a while since you had breakfast. Remember, you have to wait an hour after eating before you even think of going in the deep end. As a matter of fact, it's better to wait that long before you even go in the water."

She had told Zandy while the kids were changing that the water temperature was over ninety so it wasn't really an issue, but she still liked to play it safe.

Zandy agreed.

"Come give Mom a hug and kiss goodbye," Zandy said. "You guys behave, and, Mary, don't spoil them. Wouldn't want them to get used to it."

The boys each gave their mom her hug and kiss goodbye and then walked out to the parking lot to the car with her. By the time they got back into the motel, Mary was busy preparing grilled cheese sandwiches and tomato soup as Tom began to set the table.

"We can do that," Zaiden said. "Just show us where stuff is, and we'll take care of it."

Tom did, and the boys managed that little chore as well as cleaning up the table after meals from then on. After lunch, the boys wanted to do something while they waited for that hour to pass before they could go in the pool. Mary had them tag along with her for something to do as she showed them how she cleaned rooms when people checked out. Little did she realize then that they'd take over that little chore for the next four days.

By the time they left on Saturday morning, the three could walk into any room and have it completely refurbished for the next guest in about five minutes.

CHAPTER 17

Back at home, Zandy and the boys were getting edgy. The *couple of days* turned out to be a *couple of weeks* with no end in sight. None of Damey's trips had ever lasted that long. Between Grandpa and Grandma Williams and Zandy, they managed to keep the boys occupied, and, for the most part, sane and under control. They did everything possible to maintain the boy's normal routine so their lives weren't thrown too far out of kilter. Zandy worked from seven to four so she could get home early and fix dinner.

Like always, after school the boys would shoot baskets in the gym with their friends until Grandpa locked up and left. Then, he'd either take them to his house, or during decent weather, home, so they could swim. They had a twenty by forty foot in-ground, domed pool they used for three out of four seasons. Since they couldn't swim without an adult present, Grandpa would hang around until Zandy made it home about four-fifteen.

If the weather was not suitable for swimming, Ty would take the boys to his house, and Zandy would pick them up on the way home. The arrangement was easy because the two families only lived a couple of blocks apart. With Damey gone, Ty would also drive over in the morning and pick them up to take them to school. Everyday life for the boys wasn't all that different—except for the fact that Dad was gone, and that made the three boys grumpy and unhappy.

Zandy served dinner between five-fifteen and five-thirty, giving them plenty of time to eat, clean up the table, and then all sit down together in the living room to watch the local and national news from six to seven. Then they still took their family bike rides for close to an hour just like they always did when Dad was home.

One afternoon as the kids were headed out the kitchen door to the pool, she heard Zane mention to his brothers that their dad hadn't called for three days. Then the door closed behind them, leaving their conversation unintelligible to her. However, Zandy's ears had perked up. She'd noticed it too but hadn't said anything. She'd hoped they hadn't noticed. That wasn't like Damey. All kinds of scenarios whirled through her mind as she reached for another banana to slice up in the yogurt based fruit salad she was making.

If the kids were aware and talking about it, she knew dinner would require a little extra diligence that night to get Zack to actually eat instead of picking at his food. Of the three boys, he had taken his dad's trip to Antarctica the hardest. Getting him to eat, sleep, play, smile, or act anything that might resemble normal was getting more difficult by the day.

Zandy couldn't help but worry. His first few days there, Damey'd called almost every night around seven. He'd missed a day or two here and there, but had never missed more than two. Had something gone wrong?

When dinner was ready, she called the boys in to get dressed and set the table. They did as they were told, but were unusually quiet for them. That was not a good sign.

They all sat down and started passing bowls of food around the table.

"What's that crap?" Zack grumbled interrupting her thoughts.

"Zachary—if you can't ask appropriately, don't bother."

"Mom, how much longer is Dad gonna be gone?"

"I don't know, Honey. All I know is that not hearing from him for a couple of days makes it worse, doesn't it?"

"Three days."

Nobody said a whole lot during dinner. There was none of the usual chatter and bantering. Zandy looked around from face to face. *Damey, get your butt home. We need you.* After dinner, it took them roughly five minutes to clean everything up and start the dishwasher.

After the news, Zandy turned off the TV and told the boys, "Guys, you've got to go on your bike rides by yourselves tonight. I've got some things I need to do."

"Why? Why aren't you going with us?" Zaid asked.

"I just don't feel like it tonight, is that OK with you. Go!"

Without another word, the boys headed out the door, grabbed their bikes out of the garage, and took off for their nightly bike ride alone, which was a rarity. Their mom and dad almost always rode with them, or they didn't go at all because they either had company, it was raining, or for some other reason they were all aware of.

When they returned home, everyone settled in playing chess, reading, or checking out their iPads. The house was much quieter than normal.

Zandy's phone rang. It was in her purse where she'd dropped it on the counter when she got home from work.

Zane pulled the phone out of her purse and looked at the caller i.d. "It's Mr. Wardwell," he said walking into the living room to hand it to her.

"What's he doing calling now?" Zaiden asked. " Wow! You've been out of work for three whole hours. Can't he ever figure anything out on his own? Why's he gotta bug you now?"

As Zandy reached to take the phone from Zane , she looked at Zaiden and gave him "the look."

He shut his mouth, reddened a little, walked into the living room with his brothers, and plopped his butt on the loveseat.

Frozen in place, the three boys listened intently.

Zandy propped the phone between her shoulder and ear as she set her book on the seat beside her. "Yeah, Sam. What's up?"

She listened, nodded, said, "Uh huh" several times before ending with "Oh, no!" Before hanging up, she said, "You hear anything else, you call. I don't care what time it is. I want to know immediately."

The three boys sat or stood frozen in place, barely breathing, staring, and not moving or making a sound. Try as hard as they could, they couldn't hear a word being said on the other end.

Ending the conversation, Zandy set the phone down on the end table as all three boys circled her like vultures at a road kill yelling. "What? What? What's going on?"

"Sit!" Zandy fired back sharply as she held up her hands and motioned for them to back off.

"Just tell us, Mom. What happened?" Zack said as all three backed up and sat together on the loveseat.

"A huge, freakish storm in Antarctica left the icebreaker with major damage to its computers and generators. A fire on board destroyed a couple of the auxiliary generators so they're having problems getting things up and running again."

155

"What about Dad? Is he okay?" Zane asked.

"They're sure Dad's fine, but he's been locked into his quarters for three days, and they can't get to him for some reason. Not sure what's going on there—something freaky. Anyway, that's why we haven't heard from him."

"So that's why he hasn't called. We know he can't call from his quarters because it's encased in steel or some fool thing like that," Zane said. "That's why he always goes up on the upper deck where he has to stand out in the twenty below air to do it."

"That's right," Zandy said. "And there's not one thing we can do except carry on like normal."

Zack's paranoia took over and he went on a rant. "The icebreaker's been sabotaged, hasn't it? Somebody tried to sink the ship. Dad's gonna drown cause he can't get out of his room.

"They'll never recover his body. We'll never see him again. It's not fair. We didn't even get a chance to say goodbye."

"Oh, good grief! Don't let your imaginations play havoc with reality. Hopefully, Sam will hear more about how the situation stands tonight. At least now we know what's going on and why we haven't heard from Dad."

Zack, however, wouldn't turn it off. "Mom, are you going to send us to an orphanage? You're an unwed mother now trying to raise three kids on a single income. Please don't do that. I don't need my allowance anymore. I'll try to get a part time job to help out."

"Oh, my God. Would you knock it off? Dad is not dead. You are not orphans. I'm not sending you anyplace. We just have to wait until the Coast Guard gets this figured out."

Not admitting it to the boys, Zandy had some of the same questions milling around in her brain. She wished the boys didn't think that negatively just because she did. And would they please just shut up. All they were doing was making it harder.

Right then her phone rang again. It was Ty on the other end this time. "Hi, Dad, Sam called, and I guess now we kind of know what's going on."

She quickly went over the situation with him as the boys listened. After she finished her explanation, she asked Ty a question. "You still have that big thick belt you used to wear back in the day? Why don't you bring it over here and beat some sense into these characters? They're driving me crazy."

"Want Shaundra and I to come get them and take them out for ice cream and maybe a trip to the park for an hour or so to give you a break?"

"Yes, with lots and lots of licks," she said swinging her arm back and forth as she glared at the three of them who sat frozen with their eyes and mouths wide open.

"Mom!" they all whispered in unison when she ended the call.

"Oh, relax, and go wash your hands and faces. Grandma and Grandpa are coming over to take you out for ice cream and the park to get you out of my hair for a while."

Zane smiled. "Trying to get rid of us?"

"Yes, just for an hour or so. And, try not to drive them too nuts because you're all stressed out. Things will turn out OK. Believe me, Dad will be home soon. I know he will."

***

After they left, she walked out the pool door to sit on the patio alone so she could think. She called Sam. "Why don't you call the Department of Defense tonight and see if they would authorize my hacking into the system? I know I can get into Damey's via satellite feed. What I don't know is whether or not I can unscramble their mess or bypass it with a patch of some kind."

"All I can do is try," Sam said." I don't know if anyone in authority is around this time in the evening. However, it seems like they should be able to contact somebody who could make a decision. I'll make the call and we'll see what they say."

The next morning Zandy walked into Dewline with her brain spinning. She hadn't slept at all. She'd spent the night trying to figure out what could have gone wrong with the ship's two computers that were supposed to be running the ship.

She knew there'd be no problem connecting to Damey's computer. All she had to do was turn on his computer at work and link to the robot's. It should work flawlessly—unless, the lightning strike had fried his as well.

As usual, Sam was already there reading his emails when Zandy popped into his office. "Sam, any word from Washington yet?"

"Nope. I'll give them until ten and then call them back if I don't hear from anyone. They said last night that they were going to have the government techies try to hack into Damey's computer from their end and see if they could make his computer take over the ship. I think it's all an ego trip scenario. If you think you can do it, they figure they should be able."

"Good luck with that," Zandy said smiling. "They'll never get by Damey's personal security system. They think they're working with a bunch of amateurs?

"Yeah, I found that one a little amusing too, but I didn't say anything. I'm betting the best hacker they have can't break into his computer."

"Would you like me to reboot his and poke around a little before we get any word back from them?"

"No, if they by chance happened to be in there poking around and trying to do anything themselves, I wouldn't want to screw up any of their progress or lack of by you being in there as well—especially without their authorization. The NSA and DOD get a little picky about some things like that."

"They'd never know I was in there," Zandy said smiling, "but I'll wait. What's another hour or so at this point?"

Forty-five minutes later Sam walked up to her with a faxed document giving dual approval from both the NSA and DOD.

"All right," she said. "'bout damned time." She walked straight into Damey's office and work station and fired up his computer. Fortunately, she knew where he hid all his passwords.

"Sam, you ever see anything as ridiculous as this? Each one is a twelve digit code combining upper case and lower case letters along with numbers and symbols. I don't know where he comes up with these things. To the naked eye, none of them make any sense. They all mean something to him, though, or he'd never remember them. Ever watch him login? He never uses the cheat sheet."

Before she started, she sent a text message to Grandpa Ty at school. "Need you to 'babysit' the boys until I get home—maybe overnight. Working late. Will explain later. Important!!!"

Then she sent a text to Zack and Zaiden. Zane didn't have a phone yet as he hadn't reached his twelfth birthday. "Working late tonight. You're staying with Grandma and Grandpa. Will explain later. Tell Zane. Love you"

After the signals bounced off a satellite, she made the connection. The robot's computer seemed to be working perfectly. She made a call. The approval document had also provided cell phone contact numbers to several people on the ship. She tried Morissy first; he didn't answer.

She tried the next in line, Commander Fitz. No answer.

On her third attempt, which went to Lieutenant Commander Scott, a voice answered after the first ring.

"Commander Scott, this is Zandra Williams from Dewline Robotics Engineering in Michigan. I need to talk to Captain Morissy."

"Is this an emergency? He's sleeping."

"Wake him. I'm in control of Dr. Williams' computer as we speak. I plan to hack into your disabled computers and would like to explain to him what I'm doing first."

"Yes, Ma'am. Hold on a few minutes, please. I'll have someone go and get him."

Five minutes later Morissy showed up looking the worst for wear—unshaven, rumpled, pants, boots, and an overcoat. He looked like he'd been sleeping in his clothes. With no heat on the ship, temperatures hovered below freezing in the rooms so he probably had been.

"What's going on?" Morissy asked.

"Some lady is on the line telling me she's in control of Dr. Williams' computer and is going to hack the ship's computers and wants to talk to you."

"Give me the phone," Morissy said. "Hello. This is Captain Morissy. Who are you, and how can I be of service?"

"My name is Zandra Williams. I'm a project engineer at Dewline Robotics Engineering. I'm also the wife of Dr. Williams. Are you where you can see the monitor on Damey's computer?"

"Yes, it's right in front of me."

"Watch the arrow as I move the mouse from here. Can you see it? What's it doing?"

"It's going around in circles."

"Good. I have authorization from the NSA and the DOD to hack into your ship's computers and try to reprogram the scrambled code. Would you like me to read the document to you? Since you have no power, I can't really fax you a copy."

"No, I'll take your word for it. Good luck. We're in a bad way here."

"Okay, before I start, have you had any luck springing Damey out of his jail cell yet?"

Taken by surprise, Morissy stuttered. "No, Ma'am. We haven't been able to break the door down." He had no idea that Dewline even knew of Dr. Williams' situation.

Zandy hesitated before responding. "I have no estimated time line for how long this is going to take so we can't stay on the phone and run down your battery. Can you see the text box I'm putting on the screen? I'm putting in my number in case I need to talk to one of you."

"Yes, I see it," Morissy responded.

"Okay, if I want you to contact me, I'll send you a note underneath that says, 'Call me.' I want either you or someone else in command who is authorized to make a decision to make the call, so keep someone available. Can you see the mouse on the ship's computer monitor now?"

"Yes, that's going in circles as well."

"Good, any questions?"

"No, ma'am. We're good to go on this end. Good luck."

With that, Zandy pushed the End button on her phone and went to work.

It took a good hour before light appeared on the screen of the ship's computer. The screen was blank, but it obviously had power.

"Look," one of the seamen exclaimed. "She's typing a note in the text box on the robot's computer."

The message was short and clear, "Reboot the ship's computer."

Sean did as the rest of them gathered around the monitor and watched. Suddenly the guts of the system's programming appeared on the ship's screen—all 0s and 1s. They saw line after line of 0010110010110 and variations of the above along with other nonsensical words and symbols. None of it made any sense to those watching.

"Think she has any idea what she's doing?" Commander Scott asked Morissy.

"Beats the hell out of me. I'll guarantee you one thing, I sure as hell don't have any idea what she's doing, so I hope she does."

CHAPTER 18

Three floors below the action, and currently into the fourth day, Damey restlessly tossed and turned as he faded in and out of sleep. Periodically, he'd get out of bed, stretch, and walk back and forth and do his exercise routine just to keep the blood circulating. He felt like a bed-ridden invalid.

He wondered what they were doing topside. Apparently, they'd given up trying to break down his door. He hadn't heard a thing out there since the first day when they banged on it with something for what seemed like hours. Hopefully, they weren't going to float around the Weddell Sea waiting for someone to come and tow them back Stateside. That'd take forever and he really would starve to death.

When necessary, he'd find his way to the bathroom, but that was anything but a pleasure trip. Nasty odors permeated the place.

Having had nothing to eat or drink for a few days, the trips to the john were becoming fewer and farther between. He figured that was some kind of a positive anyway, provided he didn't dehydrate. Every few hours he'd scoop some water out of the back of the toilet tank with his hands and slurp that down, even as unappetizing as it was in there.

In the meantime, he had Zandy and the boys to worry about. He could only imagine what they were all going through. He wished he could call them.

***

With nothing better to do, those in the command center who were watching took turns walking around trying to stay semi-warm. Besides, just standing or sitting there staring at the zeros and ones as they moved around the screen was not exactly interesting or exciting after it'd been going on for hours.

Fourteen hours later almost to the minute, a note appeared on the robot's screen. "Try rebooting the ship's computer system. Don't go through the normal process. Push the power button, let it turn itself completely off, wait thirty seconds, and then turn the power back on."

Morissy looked at Sean, the seaman who normally sat behind the controls, and nodded. Sean reached down and pushed the button turning the computer off. After the screen went completely blank, he pushed the button again.

The machine whirled to life. As the screen lit up, it had gone from all the 0s and 1s to its normal startup screen. Strange sounds could be heard all over the ship—various clicking noises, snaps, strange noises from below.

They heard the generators kick in and the lights flickered on. Then, the ship shuddered as the engines roared to life.

As everyone cheered and celebrated, Morissy looked over at Ivan, Sean's work partner. "Go check on Dr. Williams."

Damey jerked awake. Squinting, he could barely open his eyes. Every light in the room had come on. His eyes felt like they were on fire. When the power first went out, Damey had made his way around the walls and flipped every switch just hoping. He blinked several times trying to adjust his focus. He used his shirtsleeves to wipe both eyes.

Aware of what must have just happened, he made his way into the latrine. He checked the faucet to see if the water had come back on. It had. Then he flushed the commode multiple times and turned on the ventilation fan. He looked into the mirror and shuddered.

With his eyes still red, watery, and stinging, he made his way to the door. Could he be that lucky?

He and Ivan reached the door at the same time. As it flew open, they looked at each other and laughed. Dirty, smelly, with multiple day beard growths, they hugged—both thankful to see the other.

"Thank God you're OK," Ivan said. "This whole thing's been a nightmare for us. I can't imagine what you've gone through."

"So, what happened anyway?"

"The ship's main computer took a direct hit by lightning and it fried everything. For some reason or the other, it left your system untouched—yet, our back up computer on the other side died in the process too. Doesn't make sense."

Damey smiled. "Yes it does. Because of the nuclear power I have running the thing, I took special care when we made it to make sure any electrical surge would flow straight through it and ground itself on whatever it was connected to. Normally, that would have been the floor. I guess in this case, it was your backup."

They slowly made their way up the steps to the main deck. After doing pretty much nothing but lie on the bed for four days and exercise when he felt like it, Damey was wobbly legged and unsteady on his feet. It took two flights of stairs before Damey loosened the death grip he had on the hand rail. They continued to talk.

"So, how'd you repair the computer? The Brass fly in a techie?" Damey asked.

"No, you ready for this?" Ivan asked. "Your wife got on your computer at Dewline, bounced a feed off a satellite, and hacked into the main computer. It took hours and hours, but she reprogrammed the damned thing, finally had us reboot it on our end, and everything came back to life. A bunch of us stood around with our mouths open watching as she kept moving the 1s and 0s from her remote site. None of us had a clue what she was doing."

"Doesn't surprise me a bit," Damey said smiling. "If anyone besides me could do it, it'd have to be her. Even the other engineers on the project back home don't know the code like she does."

When Ivan and Damey finally made it to the ship's operational station, everyone cheered. Even Morissy came up and shook his hand and expressed his relief that Damey was OK. "Your wife's a freaking genius. She hacked into your computer from stateside and fixed it. I can't believe it."

"What time is it stateside? I need to call her."

"Ah, let's see. I think it's twelve-fifteen AM yesterday back in Michigan. You said there's fifteen hours difference, didn't you?"

"Good. She got in a whole sack full of overtime if she's been working straight through. We need the money," Damey joked. "My three boys eat like they've been deprived of food for a week—sort of like I'm going to after we get everything squared away here. Cafeteria open? I sure hope so. I didn't even have a box of crackers to nibble on down there."

A couple of the seamen, pretending to take him serious about how deprived his family is, dipped their hands in their pockets and pulled out loose change and offered it to him. They all laughed. All anyone had to do was look at the rock set in gold on his right hand to know that money was not an issue in their family.

"I hope my phone's still working. I'm going to step outside in the fresh air and give Zandy a call. What's the temp out there right now?"

"Minus twenty," Morissy answered.

'Joy, joy." Damey said as he walked out the door.

The thermometer reading only told part of the story. The wind was also howling at somewhere in the vicinity of thirty knots. He didn't even want to know the windchill.

Zandy answered on the second ring. Damey could tell from the background noise that she was still at Dewline.

"My God, woman. What are you doing still there?" he asked, laughing.

"Yes, I love and miss you too," Zandy laughed. "The ship's damned computers have been up and running less than a half hour."

Their private conversation went on for several minutes—emotional for both, to say the least. She told him that his parents had the kids, so she planned on staying the rest of the night to make sure everything kept working and they were able to haul the robot and oil rig aboard without overtaxing the computers and knocking them off line again. She didn't want to get home, fall asleep, and have the phone ring needing her to race back. So, doing it this way would amount to about a forty-eight hour shift. Then she'd go home and crash until the boys got home from school.

Before they clicked off, Damey had a request. "Send Dad a text letting him know everything's OK, but ask him not to tell the boys. No sense waking them up now, they'd never get back to sleep. They'll be in school in eight hours so I'll see if I can set up some kind of conference call to surprise them. Their principal is pretty cool and might just go along with it. If not, I'll call Zack when they're all at lunch. I hope to have things pretty well wrapped up here by then."

CHAPTER 19

After ending his call to Zandy, Damey walked back into the computer room to see how things were progressing. "What's going on the with robot and oil rig?"

"Not sure," Morissy said. "When things went to hell, it was almost up to the ship. Have no idea where it is now."

"Let's take a look," Damey said as he switched the computer screen from programming to live video. "That's weird. Everything is blurry. Now what?"

Next he switched over to the radar screen. It showed the robot and oil rig within feet of the ship. The robot sat motionless while the rig swayed twenty feet below with the current.

"Know what? It's frozen in the ice. I'll try to move the thing upwards and see if I can break it free."

He adjusted the dials to raise the robot to the surface, and nothing happened. Had the nuclear battery gone dead? Had the robot been damaged from the lightning surge? He had no idea. The robot appeared to have power, but nothing moved. It had to be frozen in solid ice. Somehow they were going to have to break it free, haul it on deck, and go from there. He'd do a thorough examination of the robot when they got it back stateside.

"What're we gonna do?" Morissy asked as he watched Damey's frustration.

"Let's go get something to eat and talk about it. Think they'll let me in the cafeteria looking the way I do?"

"Four day beard growths and smelly bodies are the norm on ship today, so they'll let us in," Morissy said. "Nobody else looks any better than we do. I just hope they've got the griddle and ovens up and running by now. I'm hungry and want something hot. I can only imagine how you're feeling. At least we had dried cereal. Couldn't put milk on it though 'cause that had frozen up as well."

The menu appeared to be pretty basic when they walked into the cafeteria—fried eggs, potatoes, bacon, and toast. There was nothing gourmet, and nobody cared one bit. The place was open with a working grill and a mile-long line of people, starved for anything edible. No one on ship had eaten an actual meal in four days. Damey and Morissy waited their turns in line but didn't talk much about the situation. Neither wanted to discuss any problems with a whole line of seamen listening in.

When they got to their table and sat down, Damey told Morissy what he was thinking. "I'm guessing you don't have any equipment aboard like jackhammers where we can bust up about four feet of ice do you?"

"No, 'fraid not. That's nothing we've ever had any use for."

"OK, here's what I'm thinking. We're going to have to start up the ship and use it as a battering ram to free the robot. Once it's free, it should bob to the surface so the crew can grab it and drag it on board. The hardest part will be playing tug-of-war with the oil rig connected by that aramid fiber rope to the robot. That's floating a good twenty feet below. Thankfully, the robot's claws let loose when it lost power so we're not trying to drag the whole thing on board at the same time."

"Yeah, the robot itself took three-men-and-a-boy just to carry it over to the side when it didn't have a ton of ice clinging to it. Can't imagine what the rig weighs. Glad it's free floating below without being covered with ice. When Hector breaks loose and surfaces, we'll have to use a life boat to go out to wherever it pops up and attach a cable to it so we can haul it in. Then, if we have to, we'll line up the whole crew and drag it to the ship. The crane can haul it aboard then.

Everything went as scheduled and within five hours the robot and oil rig were both secured on the deck of the ship. Then Damey had to go back to work.

With the ship's computers still connected to Damey's, he had them plug both into regular sockets one at a time.

"Here's where it gets tricky. I want you to re-boot both computers. When you do, hopefully they will automatically switch everything from my computer to the ship's power, and then we can disconnect mine from yours. Do the main computer first, then the secondary and see what happens."

"Are we going to shut all the functions of the ship down again?" asked Morissy.

"I don't think so. Everything shut down before because of the electrical surge from the lightning. I think all the generators and engines will continue to work normally even if we turn off the computers. Let's hope for the best. Go for it and see what happens."

Ivan looked at Damey, paused, wiped a little sweat off his brow, and ran through the reset procedure. Nothing changed.

"OK, now do the backup," Damey said.

Same results—no change.

"Disconnect the main computer from mine and connect it to the other one."

Again, nothing changed. All lights, power, and engines continued to run flawlessly.

"I am going to shut mine down and leave it in position and just watch things for a while. If nothing bad happens for a couple of hours, we'll crate it up and call for transport. Have you arranged for someone to pick up the oil rig and ship it back to DC yet?"

"No, not yet," Morissy said. "Guess we can do that now. I'm betting they'll send two planes. I've got a sneaking suspicion they won't want anyone to know exactly where they take this thing—even you. I would assume they'll pick you up with a separate plane at McMurdo and ship you, your computer, and Hector nonstop to Michigan."

Damey smiled when Morissy referred to his robot by the name the Zs had given it.

Damey kept an eye on his watch. Zandy had given him the school's office number, and he'd put it in his contact list. At nine AM *home time* he took out his phone, went over to the edge of the cabin for privacy, and pushed the little green icon that called the school.

By then all of the student aides who normally answered the phone to record absences were gone to class so the school's secretary, who'd been there for over forty years and remembered Damey from his own school days, answered.

"Hi, Mrs. Murphy. This is Damey Williams. Can you patch me through to Mr. Rogers? I need to talk to him right now if that's possible."

"Thank God you're OK. Your three kids are walking basket cases, and Ty isn't much better. Hold on one second. I'm not hanging up; I'm putting you on hold. I've got to drag him out of the hall."

Thirty seconds later the line clicked on again as Rogers spoke. "Dr. Williams. Is it really you? Your kids all have you drowned at sea a gazillion miles away. What can I do?"

"I was beginning to wonder myself. It's a long story that I can't say anything about unless it hits the news. In the meantime, can you get Dad and the three boys somewhere secure and hopefully soundproof where I can talk to them on speaker phone? None of them know that I've been freed from my *little* situation. I want to surprise them."

"OK, I think I can get them down here pretty quickly. I won't tell any of them about what is going on except that they have someone calling them with news about you from where?"

"Tell them it's from a Coast Guard Icebreaker 'cause that's what I'm on, and they do know that much."

"Hold on. I'm putting you back on hold. When I come back on live, they'll be here and, we'll be on speaker phone."

Rogers hustled into the main office and grabbed the microphone on the school's PA system, turned up the volume a little higher than normal, and pushed the button. "May I have your attention, please? Sorry to interrupt, but I have an emergency message that I need to relay. I need the following people to come to my office immediately. I need Mr. Tyrone Williams, Zachary, Zaiden, and Zane Williams. Boys, you have my permission to run. I want you here, *NOW*. "

Ty was close. First hour was his planning period, and he was in the teacher's lounge right across the hall. Zandy hadn't texted him like Damey had suggested. She decided to make it a four-way surprise when the call came through. Keeping a straight face, Mr. Rogers told him to stand there in front of the desk. Forty-five seconds later the third boy burst through the door out of breath.

Rogers motioned them all up to the desk and then spoke. "The four of you have an official group telephone communication from a US Coastguard Icebreaker someplace with some important information about Dr. Williams. Hold on while I answer the call on speaker phone."

That was dirty trick, and he knew it. The boys stood there trembling and Ty didn't look in much better shape. He caught Ty's eye with a slight grin and furtive wink. Ty took a deep breath and relaxed.

Rogers pushed the button on the phone. "Sir, the four individuals you requested to speak with are currently standing in front of the speaker phone. As

soon as you begin, and I know the connection is
working, I will leave the room."

After about a five second pause, Damey spoke.
"Are you sure my dad and three sons are in that room?
I've never heard it this quiet when the four of them are
together."

Unfortunately for anyone in the vicinity, the room
was not soundproofed, and it was an ear buster. The
screams and voices echoed off the walls. Rogers
walked into the main office wiping his eyes with his
handkerchief. He looked at Mrs. Murphy. "Guess who
isn't dead and buried at sea after all?"

She couldn't answer. She did what came naturally;
she got up and headed for the ladies' room blowing her
nose.

Damey wasn't sure what actual news if any had
made it through and what hadn't. So, he told them that
Mom had been the one to free him, but he didn't think
it registered. They were all yelling, laughing, crying,
and talking at the same time. He tried to make the point
for his dad to call his mom and let her know too, but
wasn't sure if the message got through or not with all
the noise. Didn't matter, he knew he'd do it anyway.
After a half hour, the uproar dulled to the point that he
could get the message through to all that he would be
home soon. He hoped it'd be in the next couple of days.

CHAPTER 20

After he finished with his phone call, he looked at Morissy. "I'm going to go lie down for a while, take a shower, shave and try to feel human again. If anything bad or unexpected happens, come and get me,"

Damey walked into his room, which was still fully lit and back to normal. He managed to turn off some lights and kick off his shoes before flopping face first onto the bed. He went out like a flicked-off light bulb himself. For the first time since he'd been there, he didn't dream of home. In fact, he didn't dream of anything.

Several hours later, he stood in front of the mirror, shaving and thinking. How weird was that, he thought to himself. The least I could have done was have one last dream about our trip to Disney World. I think that's the only major thing we did last summer that I missed. He smiled thinking about it.

After his shower and clean clothes, Damey realized he was starving again. He wondered if the kitchen had gone back to normal yet. He'd like a regular meal.

He walked back on deck and checked the monitors. Everything had continued to work perfectly. Morissy stood there with a strange look on his face. "You hungry? We need to talk."

After they'd gone through the line and picked up their roast beef dinner, they sat down. "What's up?" Damey asked.

"While you were asleep a helicopter came and picked up the oil rig and hauled it back to McMurdo. There is a transport plane already in route to pick it up and take it back to the DC area."

"The copter coming back to get me then?"

"No, that's the problem. The State Department wants you to stay here until they've had a chance to inspect the rig. If they decide it's pre-1988 and harmless, they'll come and get you. If it's relatively new, they want you to send Hector back under the ice cap to see if you can find anything else going on."

"Oh, boy! That's going to go over big on the home front. I can hear the Zs now. How long are they expecting this to take?"

"It'll take at least twenty-four hours getting it to the inspection site. They hope they'll be able to determine what its status is within a day or so."

"So, what the hell am I supposed to do while I wait? Sit around and stare at the monitors?"

"Nope. Thanks to Mrs. Williams, everything is working perfectly just like nothing happened. Spend your time in the dayroom, cafeteria, or wherever. You know, a lot of the crewmen are dying to meet and talk with you. It'd be great for morale if you did.

"We're going to hang in the area right here until we're cleared, and then we'll be headed out as well. I think when we leave, we'll be headed back to the States for decommissioning. This thing is so old and obsolete, it's not worth keeping in operation. So, I guess your main chore is to keep the battery charged on your phone and call home as often as you can."

***

Almost a month to the day after Damey left, Zandy and the boys were watching the six o'clock news they always watched. In the middle of the weather forecast, the regular announcer broke in. "Breaking News, an oil spill has been discovered in the Antactica, and an underwater robot has been deployed to stop the leak. No further details are reported at that time."

That was old news as far as they were concerned. Zandy flipped channels to CNN knowing they'd have the latest. There was none of the normal chatter and discussion about various news events among them. The four of them sat rigidly and expressionless as they stared at the screen. The national news channel expected to have further information and interviews by eleven.

"Mom, we have to stay up and watch that. Maybe they'll interview Dad."

"No way. You're going to bed at your regular times like always. This is a school night."

"Mom!" all three yelled at the same time.

"Whatever is said, you'll hear about it tomorrow. No arguments. Just sleep well tonight knowing Dad is safe and will be home soon."

"Yeah, but they're making him stay there until they inspect the rig," Zack growled. "Not fair. Isn't he ever going to come home? He's been gone forever."

After dropping the boys off at the door and then parking his car in the teacher's parking lot out behind the gym, Ty stopped by the Principal's office. "Think there's anything you can do? The Zs are beside themselves this morning. 'Mom wouldn't let 'um stay up.' You should've heard the whining on the way to school. What made it worse, of course, is the fact that the primary person interviewed was Damey via a satellite Skype. He didn't have a whole lot to say that we didn't already know. What's driving the kids nuts is they haven't let him leave yet. When they do, it'll be another twenty-four hours or so before he gets home. Hopefully, that'll be soon. Sounds like they've determined that it's an old, old rig, or they wouldn't have announced it."

"Let me see what I can do. Can't promise anything."

What Ty and the principal knew, and most people didn't because it was never advertised for a lot of obvious reasons, was that the superintendent of schools was related to a CNN executive. Mr. Rogers put in a call.

That afternoon at the beginning of the last hour, an announcement came over the loud speaker. "May I have your attention, please? As you all know by now, an oil leak in the Antarctica was located in the past weeks and sealed. CNN showed an exclusive interview via Skype at eleven o'clock last night with Dr. Damarian Williams who headed up the search and repair mission. As we have Dr. Williams' father and three sons here at our school, the station graciously sent us a copy of the full interview. It takes about twenty minutes. I am going to play it now."

With that, all of the classroom television sets popped on and the program began. Zack sat in Mr. Allen's Algebra class with his eyes glued to the screen. Mr. Allen and Mr. Williams along with Mrs. Murphy were the last remaining personnel left from the Damey era. In fact, Mr. Allen had been the one who broke up a fight that involved Damey after a bullying incident years previously. He wondered if Damey had ever told the boys about it. Probably not. He'd never heard it mentioned.

A steady flow of tears dripped off of Zack's chin puddling on the desk. He never wiped his cheeks or moved a muscle as he stared at the screen unaware that more kids were watching him in silence than the TV.

Towards the end of the interview, the announcer asked Dr. Williams what was the most impressive thing to him about the whole operation.

"Without a doubt the real hero of this whole operation is my wife, Zandy, back at Dewline. She worked for twenty-six hours straight hacking into my computer here on ship, and from there hacking into the ship's computers while she reprogrammed them back to life. Without her, I'd probably still be locked into a storage room three floors below the surface."

Zack's eyes and mouth flew open. Mom saved Dad? It had never registered. After all the crap he'd given her just because he was stressed, Zack knew his face flushed crimson. Feeling embarrassed would be an understatement.

Even though their dad had told them, none of the boys had realized the fact. Things had been way too hectic when that call came through.

Lastly, the newscaster asked, "Do you plan to stay until the rest of the mission is completed which the Department of Defense said could take a couple more weeks?"

"No, I'm ready to clear out of here as soon as the Coast Guard gets a plane here to take me and my equipment back. In the meantime, we can monitor anything that might be needed from home via our

satellite computer hookup. Thanks to Zandy, I don't
need to be physically on site anymore. Besides, I have a
number of other important projects I'm working on that
I have to be there for—namely, monitoring the Z-
Team."

"Oh? Can you tell us anything about that one?
Sounds important."

"Sorry, that's classified."

At that point, the class heard nothing more from the
television because Zack wailed loud enough to drown it
out. "Stop talking and come home. I can't stand having
you gone anymore."

With that he dropped his head to his desk cradled by
both arms and sobbed.

"Jesse," Mr. Allen said," would you run fast down
to the gym and get Mr. Williams. He has a class going
on, but tell him he's got to come. Hurry!"

Jesse shot out of the room and ran down the hall.
Ironically, he was Zack's best friend and son of
Damey's best friend, Alex. Damey and Alex had been
best buddies since middle school.

Halfway there, Jesse spotted Tyrone walking
rapidly in his direction. "Grandpa, come quick. Zack
needs you bad."

"I was afraid of that. Is he having a melt down?"

"More like a crash and burn."

There were thirty-four kids in the school who all
considered themselves cousins, and Ty and Shaundra

were one of their sets of grandparents. They were not only the offspring of Damey and Zandy,, but also the other ten kids who had hung out together twenty-five or six years previously and had remained best friends throughout the years.

Ty broke into a jog wondering, *am I going to have to deal with boys going through puberty forever?* I'm getting too old for this. When I get all these kids through middle school, I'm going to retire.

When he reached the room, he slipped through the door and sat down in Jesse's seat beside Zack. He put his arm around his grandson and whispered in his ear.

Zack whirled around, buried his head in his grandpa's neck, and cried even harder. Ty held him tightly and continued to whisper in his ear as he rocked him gently until he could get Zack to slide over and slip out the door with him. Keeping his arm around him, he led him down to the boy's bathroom.

With that start to the class period, Mr. Allen told the kids to find something to study. No way could he carry on with the day's lesson plan.

Then he called Zaid and Zane's teachers to let them know where they could find their grandfather and Zack if they needed them. They did. The boys clung to Grandpa in the boy's room until they got it out of their systems. The stress had finally gotten the best of them.

Five minutes or so before the end of the period, Zack returned—looking somber, but dry eyed. He sat down in his seat, looked around at all the kids trying to ignore him but still sneaking peeks, and raised his hand.

"What, Zack," Mr. Allen said.

"Can I say something to the class?" he said in barely more than a whisper.

"I guess."

Zack looked around the room noticing all eyes were on him. "I just wanted to apologize for ruining the whole class for everyone. I know you didn't do anything for Mr. Allen today 'cause you're all working on different stuff."

Across the room next to the windows, one of his *cousins*, Layla, pushed back her chair and stood with her hands on her hips and yelled. "Zachary Berkley Williams, don't you *dare* apologize for missing your dad so much you can't stand it. That is just *so* wrong."

The class clapped and shouted as they jumped out of their seats voicing their agreement.

"Wait, wait, stop," Zack said holding up his arms. "You're gonna get me goin' again."

Everyone laughed out loud breaking the tension— even Zack for the first time in almost a month.

The bell rang.

***

That afternoon after school, Ty had a doctor's appointment so he dropped the boys off at Dewline for Zandy to keep tabs on until she went home at four. As they slammed the cars doors shut and raced for the building, he felt a little guilty relief. He was rid of their adolescent paranoia for the afternoon.

It was never any problem dropping them off because they were all so interested in the robots. Any time he had other things he needed to do, that's what he did. Then they would spend their afternoons with the engineers pestering them with questions.

This time, however, was different. They raced to Zandy's office and literally attacked her with hugs, love, and apologies. Why hadn't she told them? The reaction from the three of them took her back a little. She hadn't expected that.

"Boys, I really didn't want to say anything about my part in the operation because our main concern was Dad, not what I was doing. The important thing is he's free and on his way home."

After that, she shooed them out of her office because she had a couple of loose ends to tie up before leaving for the day. When it was time to go home, she looked for the boys. They were nowhere in sight.

"Where are the boys?" she asked one of the engineers they usually followed aroun.

"They went into Mr. Wardwell's office right after they left your office," the engineer said. "The door's been closed all this time. Said there was something they wanted to talk with him about—college or something like that."

"Oh, no," Zandy muttered under her breath. She buzzed Sam. When he answered, she told him, "Tell the boys it's time for us to go home."

When the door opened, they were all smiling and said goodbye to each other. Zandy thought that was a good sign.

"What was that all about?" Zandy asked thinking back on the Winter Break explosion.

"Nothing, we were just talking," Zaid responded.

Thursday morning Zandy, the boys, Grandpa and Grandma, Sam Wardwell, a group of Dewline employees, and reporters gathered on the tarmac at the Capitol City International Airport waiting for Damey's plane to land.

"There it is," Zane yelled as a huge cargo plane passed north of the runway to line up for landing.

True to their nature, all three boys excitedly started talking at the same time. Zandy looked at Ty and Shaundra and smiled. They *kind of* were able to follow the kid's jabbering. Most people couldn't. Didn't matter. *Everyone* was happy again.

When the plane finally touched down, the whole family cheered. They couldn't wait. As the huge cargo transport taxied into position and shut down her engines, everyone edged closer and closer. A barrier had been set up, but they seemed to be able to slide it forward more than security would have liked.

When Damey departed the plane, the boys burst under the barrier and ran for their dad. They all but tackled him on the tarmac. The rest of the family came running hot on their tails. Hugs and kisses abounded and even a tear or two or three.

As they started to drift towards the terminal, a reporter shouted a question. "Dr. and Mrs. Williams, we'd like to interview the two of you. Can we do it now?"

"Not right now. I've got to go over to Dewline and make sure the robot is secured and checked out. We had a slight problem that needs to be looked at," Damey said looking over his shoulder.

Wild-eyed and half panic stricken, Zack caught Sam's eye as he mouthed, "NO!"

Sam held up his index finger for Zack to hold on a minute, winked at him, and said to the reporters, "Excuse me, but you're going to have to wait until Monday to interview the Williams'. In the meantime, I do have an announcement you may be interested in. During Dr. Williams' absence, I had a long meeting with our board of directors, and after ruminating a few days on the concerns of the most vociferous one of the group, I have decided it's time for me to be going into semi-retirement as CEO of Dewline. On Monday, Dr. Williams takes over as president of the company. I don't know how we'll manage everything, but the other engineers are going to have to take over his duties as our roving troubleshooter for all offsite problems that arise in the future.

"Now, if you have any more questions that I can address, fine. I'll take them. However, Dr. and Mrs. Williams are going to gather up their brood and get out of my sight. If I catch any one of the five of them within a mile of Dewline before Monday morning, I'm might decide I have to fire the whole bunch of them."

Zack burst into nearly hysterical laughter. He literally bounced up and down on his toes with every tooth in his mouth showing, "If you fire us all, does that mean I won't have to get a double doctorate in robotics engineering and law after all?"

Sam tried to frown but couldn't pull it off. Instead, with a huge grin of his own, the two of them made eye-contact as he raised both hands and waved them towards the gate. "Get out of here!"

Damey's eyes swiveled between Sam and Zack wondering what was going on. *What the hell is he talking about? He's named me president of the company? Why? I don't get it. What's happened while I've been gone? I won't be going on any more of these excursions? Good, but we don't even have a board of directors—much less a vociferous one. Who's he been talking to?*

Then, the sunlight peeked over the horizon in his brain, "ZACK!"

THE END

If you liked *Damey & the Z-Team,* you also may enjoy *Damey & Grandpa Tutor* which takes place twenty-six years earlier when Damey was a boy.

Damey & Grandpa Tutor

Gathered with his adoptive great uncles for the official reading of Grandpa's will, Damey's mind drifted back fourteen years.

Moving into a Habitat for Humanity's home across from William (Bill) Berkley, a retired secondary school teacher, turned into the first good break in Damey's life. Bill stepped in to be his tutor, mentor, friend, confidant, and eventual adoptive grandpa.

Damey and his best buddy, Alex, teamed up for games and adventures—including the time where the two found themselves lost in the woods after following a pure white deer. One cannot stay lost for long before nature calls. Damey cleaned himself using green, three-pronged leaves found in the woods—poison ivy. Sometimes, RediCares do not concern themselves with patient modesty.